THE FORTUNES OF TEXAS

*Follow the lives and loves of a complex family
with a rich history and deep ties
in the Lone Star State*

SECRETS OF FORTUNE'S GOLD RANCH

Welcome to Fortune's Gold Ranch...where the vistas of Emerald Ridge are as expansive as the romantic entanglements that beckon its visitors!

CONVENIENTLY A FORTUNE

Business student Jacinta Gomez is tantalizingly close to realizing her dreams of revitalizing her grandmother's chocolate factory until her *abuela* delivers an ultimatum: *Find a husband... or the business will never be yours!* When her boss, Micah Fortune, steps in with a practical one-year-marriage proposal, it's a win-win proposition. That is, until their pesky hearts get in the way...

Dear Reader,

I've been writing for Harlequin for twenty-five years now, and for the first time ever, it's my great pleasure to share with you my debut in the Fortunes of Texas series. I'm so delighted to be a part of this great group of romances, especially as I was able to write about one of my favorite things: chocolate. Seriously, whenever anyone asks me what my favorite food is, the answer is always chocolate.

Jacinta knows about chocolate, too. It's more than the subject of her MBA—it's her passion. She's determined to take over her family business and bring it to the next level. The only problem is that her grandmother wants her married. Enter Micah Fortune, CEO extraordinaire and Jacinta's mentor and boss. He's involved in a family situation that brings his maturity and ability to take on more responsibility into question. And he can't help but see a solution to both his and Jacinta's problems—they get married. In name only. Trouble is, he's very attracted to her, and she him, and she's in his kitchen making chocolate...

I loved writing this marriage-of-convenience story. For research, I even visited a local chocolate manufacturer and toured the factory with one of the owners, who sent me home with, you guessed it, chocolate. As part of your reading experience, I highly suggest keeping a few chocolate truffles nearby.

Enjoy,

Michele

CONVENIENTLY
A FORTUNE

MICHELE DUNAWAY

THE FORTUNES OF TEXAS

Special thanks and acknowledgment are given to
Michele Dunaway for her contribution to
The Fortunes of Texas: Secrets of Fortune's Gold Ranch miniseries.

Harlequin®
THE FORTUNES OF TEXAS

Recycling programs for this product may not exist in your area.

ISBN-13: 978-1-335-99681-7

Conveniently a Fortune

Copyright © 2025 by Harlequin Enterprises ULC

Harlequin Enterprises ULC
22 Adelaide St. West, 41st Floor
Toronto, Ontario M5H 4E3, Canada
www.Harlequin.com

Printed in Lithuania

MIX
Paper | Supporting responsible forestry
FSC® C021394

In first grade, **Michele Dunaway** wanted to be a teacher. In second grade, she wanted to be a writer. By third grade, she decided to be both. Now a bestselling author, Michele strives to create strong heroes and heroines for savvy readers who want contemporary, small-town adventures with characters who discover things about themselves as they travel the road to true love and self-fulfillment. Michele loves to travel, with the places she visits often inspiring her novels. An avid baker, Michele describes herself as a woman who does way too much but never wants to stop, especially when it comes to creating fiction, or baking brownies and chocolate chip cookies. She loves to hear from readers at micheledunaway.com.

Books by Michele Dunaway

The Fortunes of Texas: Secrets of Fortune's Gold Ranch

Conveniently a Fortune

Harlequin Special Edition

Love in the Valley

What Happens in the Air
All's Fair in Love and Wine
Love's Secret Ingredient
One Suite Deal
Room for Two More

Visit the Author Profile page
at Harlequin.com for more titles.

For Christina Abel, merci. To Guy, Judy and Marty because I can't believe I haven't put my siblings in a dedication yet. And to Richard, Olivia Sigal and Oreo for spoiling me, merci beaucoup.

Chapter One

In hindsight, it was the talk of conveyor belts and cooling machinery that ended up being the final proverbial straw figuratively breaking the camel's back. Or if Jacinta Gomez was being literal, it was the very mention of the topic of how to increase candy production that caused her seventy-five-year-old grandmother to issue what would be later known as "the ultimatum."

The timing of the discussion hadn't been the problem. Jacinta had broached the subject of expansion while packaging solid chocolate Easter rabbits. As part of her MBA capstone course, Jacinta had developed the perfect business plan as to how Abuela Rosa Chocolates could go from one line of production into four, and she'd been warming to the topic when her grandmother—the company owner and the very Abuela Rosa who'd raised her since she was six—had started waving a finger and shaking her hairnet-covered head. Then she had said her granddaughter needed to find a husband.

"Husband first. Business second," Rosa had snapped and, aware of the curious and amused expressions of her grandmother's two part-time workers, Jacinta had bitten her lip and dropped the subject.

Her abuela's quest to find her a husband was nothing

new. Married herself by twenty-one, with her beloved son married to Jacinta's mother at age twenty-two, Rosa Gomez defined matriarch. To Abuela, Jacinta's age was a liability. At twenty-six years old, Jacinta was over the hill. Out to pasture. Sitting on a shelf. As a modern woman, Jacinta found Abuela's ideas of marrying young old-fashioned and quaint. While Rosa was one hundred percent Mexican, as was Jacinta's late father, the Gomez family was also one hundred percent American and born in Texas, same as Jacinta herself. Her family was proof positive of the power of the American Dream.

As for marriage? Jacinta's generation was marrying later, to Abuela's consternation. Jacinta had bigger dreams and goals, ones that did not include finding Mr. Right or even Mr. Right Now. She would graduate in May with her MBA. Besides the independent study capstone, part of her program included an administrative assistant internship. She worked for Micah Fortune, CEO of the Fortune's Gold Ranch cattle operation, a multimillion-dollar working ranch that came complete with a fancy spa and guest hotel incorporated into the property. All of the Fortune siblings and cousins worked in the family's various ranch-related businesses.

While her boss—who'd insisted she call him Micah—lived on the ranch, his offices were on the second floor of an ornate limestone, eight-floor building in downtown Emerald Ridge. Jacinta was one of ten or so employees who worked in town. Her coworkers included an IT manager, an accountant, the sales team and a human resources officer. She enjoyed her internship, which not only paid well but allowed her to meet some of Emerald Ridge's prominent business owners and the state's most influential leaders.

Nevertheless, Jacinta's true love was chocolate, which

was why she'd brought up expanding Abuela Rosa Chocolates. Her grandmother's chocolate was exceptional and in high demand. In fact, because of her limited production capabilities, Abuela had had to close the Easter ordering a week early. Jacinta, the two part-timers and her abuela had been working since 7:00 a.m. that morning. They'd almost finished packaging the orders, which was good considering the holiday was occurring next week.

Excited about what she'd developed for her MBA, Jacinta couldn't help but share the ideas she'd been putting into her independent study capstone project, which was a business plan for Abuela Rosa Chocolates. After all, the demand was there.

Her college professors encouraged Jacinta to follow her vision. She saw a way to keep the quality of the handcrafted chocolates while also expanding both the company's online presence and production itself. For starters, Abuela Rosa Chocolates could be the exclusive chocolate supplier to the exclusive, luxe guest ranch and spa at Fortune's Gold Ranch.

Before her grandmother cut her off, Jacinta had been explaining her research, detailing how the Abel family, now in its second generation, had expanded their Chocolate Chocolate Chocolate Company beyond St. Louis into a national brand. The Abel family's holdings included Bissinger's, one of the longest standing names in the confection industry.

But instead of responding with enthusiasm, Jacinta had watched her five-foot-one grandmother's full lips pucker. After the pointing, finger-shaking and husband-finding declaration, her abuela didn't mince words, saying, "You. Me. We talk later."

Later was *never* a good thing. Jacinta had learned that fact early, like that one time in third grade when, wanting the latest popular girl style, she'd cut her long, black hair with Abuela's best fabric scissors. Her grandmother had said she'd fix the damage to Jacinta had done to her hair later. Two days of attending school with her hair chopped erratically had taught Jacinta the lesson Abuela had wanted her to learn, which was to ask adults for help before doing radical things. She'd never cut her hair since, minus getting professional salon trims from her first cousin Sofia. Jacinta rarely curled her hair, preferring to part her black hair in the middle and let the straight strands fall to her midback. That was, when the strands weren't tucked into a hairnet like the one she currently wore.

"Okay, later," Jacinta replied, hiding her irritation at Abuela's immediate dismissal of her ideas.

Her abuela nodded. "I'm leaving you. I need to cook. Family arrives at six." With that, she left the two-car garage that had been converted before Jacinta was born into a chocolate creation workspace, leaving her and the two part-timers to finish packaging the chocolates and readying them for pickup.

Jacinta set aside some pieces of broken Easter bunny chocolate. One of her ideas that had been incorporated was that nothing should go to waste. Broken or imperfect pieces would be bagged and sold for a discount, and Abuela had a steady clientele for those specials.

"Almost done, Jacinta," one of the workers called. "Saul texted that he's almost here to pick up the orders."

"Excellent." She studied the interior of the two-car garage that the business had outgrown. If they had double the space, they could create even more of the chocolate confections that were made from top-secret recipes passed down for generations. Jacinta's favorites were the chocolate-covered caramels and chocolate-covered Oreo cookies. Others loved the chocolate-covered strawberries, which were a year-round staple.

How many customers had Abuela turned away this spring holiday season? Too many, which bothered Jacinta greatly. Once outside the production facility, she removed her hairnet and shook her long hair free. When it came to change, her grandmother was stubborn. She crossed the small backyard and entered the kitchen. "Saul's picking up the orders now," Jacinta said.

"Thank you for letting me know." Abuela pulled a tray of enchiladas from the oven. Unlike the kind that were smothered in cheese sauce and baked as a casserole, her grandmother used an old family recipe to make her red sauce by hand. The kitchen smelled of the garlic and oregano, which had been added to the guajillo peppers and the ancho peppers Abuela deseeded and roasted herself.

Jacinta knew the recipe by heart, for years having watched as her abuela would dip each corn tortilla in the red sauce, fry it and then fill the tortilla with either a beef or chicken mixture. Tonight's enchiladas, like always, would be served with a sprinkled cheese and garnished with cubed potatoes and carrots that had first been boiled and then fried in the same pan used for the corn tortillas.

Palm Sunday dinner was in full swing as Jacinta took her seat at the dining room table, which had been handcrafted by her *bisabuelo*. Her woodworker great-grandfather had died before she was born, but she'd heard all the stories. Family heritage was important to Abuela, which is why tonight the entire family surrounded the table for dinner at the holidays, as well as almost every Sunday.

Abuela sat at the head of the table. Her brother, Jacinta's eighty-year-old great-uncle Luis, was at the opposite end. Jacinta secured a spot next to her second cousin Roberto, who preferred to be called Rob, not that the old-fashioned Abuela ever would shorten his name despite his requests. Across the table were Jacinta's first cousin Sofia and her husband Dan. Sofia had married at twenty-two and, eight years later, had two children who were eating in the family room. Kaitlyn Maria was seven and in second grade and Jackson Carlos was six and in kindergarten. Sofia's parents—Abuela's daughter and son-in-law—lived in L.A. While they visited often, they would not make it for Easter.

"How's the salon?" Jacinta asked as she served herself. Sofia owned one of Emerald Ridge's better salons. Her husband worked for the Fortunes as the maintenance supervisor for the Fortune's Gold Guest Ranch and Spa.

Sofia swallowed a bird-sized bite of enchilada. "Great. Doing well. You know, your hair is long enough to cut more than a half inch. You could make good money selling it."

"Thanks for the offer, but I like it this length," Jacinta said. That was her cousin, who lately appeared to be counting every dime and seemed abnormally stressed. Maybe it was because she had her kids in private school. Or because Dan seemed to be out at the ranch nonstop. Jacinta bowed her head as Uncle Luis said grace. After dinner, dessert was homemade flan. Jacinta was midway through her first bite, and enjoying how the pistachio flavor mixed with the custard and crystalized sugar, when her abuela tapped her spoon on her water glass.

"I have something to say." As everyone turned their heads, Abuela folded her hands. Jacinta frowned. Was her hair grayer? Or the line crossing her forehead deeper? Surely, her grandmother wasn't going to say anything terrible had befallen her, like cancer. Jacinta's stomach churned. Abuela was seventy-five. Still young at heart. Spry.

"As you know, chocolate is more than a hobby for me.

It's about family. It's about perfecting and using a recipe as a way to remember and honor those who came before us, who paved the way for our family to prosper. Making chocolate is about more than the end result or how many varieties I create. It's about the love and care our family puts into each individual piece and the happiness eating our chocolate brings to others."

Hearing this didn't help Jacinta relax. She knew all this already. In fact, Abuela had stressed the legacy from the moment Jacinta had first stood on a stool holding a wooden spoon.

Abuela gazed around the table, her expression loving yet somber. "All I've wanted is for my family to be happy and fulfilled. Thus, I've decided to move on from running the business."

Jacinta's surprised gasp joined everyone else's. *"Abuela!"* she said. Why hadn't her grandmother said something in private? She'd told Jacinta that her goal was for her to take the reins one day, hence the MBA and the business plan.

"When will this happen?" Sofia asked. "Are you selling?"

Her grandmother waved a hand and everyone fell silent. "My greatest legacy sits at this table. You, my beloved family. That is why I say this before everyone sitting here tonight…"

Jacinta's stomach clenched. From her grandmother's tone, it didn't sound like she was handing over the company. "What exactly are you trying to say?"

Abuela turned to Jacinta and took her granddaughter's hand. She squeezed lightly and the knots in Jacinta's stomach tightened. "Jacinta, you know I want you to have the company. But family matters. That is why I say this before everyone sitting before us tonight. If you are not married by the time your work-study program ends, then I am giving the company to Sofia."

Her cousin grabbed her husband's hand before he tugged it from her grasp. "Abuela! That is so generous! You know Dan and I will keep the legacy exactly as it is."

From her dramatic gushing, Jacinta could tell Sofia didn't intend to do anything of the sort. Stung, Jacinta recoiled and shoved her hands into her lap. "Abuela," she protested, everything inside her working not to scream. The words still came out louder than intended. "That's not even seven weeks from now. How can you do this to me?"

"Do not disrespect your elders," Uncle Luis said before Jacinta could add "to my dream."

"Sorry," Jacinta mumbled. She flicked her gaze to the white tablecloth. How much additional humiliation could she stand?

Abuela turned in her direction and Jacinta lifted brown eyes so similar to those of her grandmother's. "I know you don't understand, *mi querida*, but you've been unwed long enough. I run my company without having a fancy degree. I made chocolate while raising *tu papa*, bless his soul. Family, Jacinta, and the love of a good man are what you need. I don't want to take things from you, and this might be a painful lesson. But life is more than work, work, work. It's heritage and love. I want you to find that."

Jacinta bit her lip, the pain keeping her from saying anything more. When her grandmother made a decision, it was final. Having lost her appetite, she pushed the rest of her uneaten flan away.

Never had she been so blindsided or put into an impossible situation. To get her grandmother's company, she needed a man. Stat. She huffed out a frustrated breath. No one forced people to get married in this decade, did they? Women were raised to set goals and achieve dreams.

Abuela Rosa Chocolates was a birthright promise. Ever

since her grandmother had taught her the secret recipes, Jacinta had dreamed of the moment she'd make the company her own. She'd wanted nothing else. At eight, she had been stirring butter, cream and salt into melted sugar to make caramel. By ten, she'd been creating chocolate and pouring it over sandwich cookies. And by twelve? She'd graduated to filling molds. Being a chocolatier was her passion. If she had her way, Abuela Rosa Chocolates would be a nationwide, handcrafted brand that promised its purchasers excellent and great memories in every bite.

But her grandmother's stance—arms stubbornly folded across her matronly, full-figured chest—meant that to own Abuela Rosa Chocolates, and to see those dreams into fruition, Jacinta needed a husband.

By May 31. Or else.

Jacinta knew her grandmother operated from the best of intentions, as she had ever since she'd taken an orphaned Jacinta in to raise. Her grandmother's heart was in the right place, but the decision was not. But barring a miracle, Abuela would not see reason or back down. Fuming, Jacinta tapped her fingers against her thighs, tuning out Sofia's jabbering about running the company. No matter what, she refused to lose her opportunity to make her mark in the world. Her cousin might be married with children, but Sofia's interest in the family chocolate business ended with the minuscule profit sharing their grandmother did every December.

Not that the company was that profitable. Its small, loyal following kept it afloat and in the black. Jacinta had never understood why Abuela hadn't expanded beyond the reach of their hometown of Emerald Ridge, Texas. In these days of internet sales, the future was unlimited. But no, Abuela stayed true to a town whose give-or-take-a-few-ten-thousand people were outnumbered three-to-one by the cattle grazing on the surrounding ranches.

"I know you're not happy, *mi amada nieta*, but this is how it must be. You're twenty-six. I'd had your father in kindergarten by the time I was your age. He was the light of my life. Life is too short." Abuela loosened her arms and crossed herself. "Way too short."

Jacinta hardly remembered her parents. They'd died in a car crash when she was young. Everyone said she looked like her mother: same long dark hair, almond-shaped, light brown eyes, high cheekbones and straight nose. People had always maintained she could have been a model—except for her five-foot-four height was that of her mother and her abuela, not from her father who'd topped six feet.

"Jacinta, if you'd like, I could play matchmaker," Sofia offered. "Dan has some single friends who work at the ranch."

Matchmaking was the *last* thing Jacinta wanted. When he wasn't at work, Dan was often out doing something, leaving Sofia alone to juggle her kids and her career. Jacinta desired a man who would be an equal partner. Even if her standards made her appear picky, she was not lowering them. She was choosy, as her girlfriend Kim had said. But Kim had reinforced that it was okay to be selective in your soulmate.

"Thanks, but I'm fine," Jacinta said. "I'll figure it out."

"Are you even dating?" Sofia asked, knowing the answer was no.

"I'm fine," she repeated, letting herself be as stubborn as Abuela. Sure, she'd dated, but she'd often ended things because her partners wanted something beyond what she was prepared to give. They'd demand more of her time, and whine about why she didn't want to go beyond kissing.

Surely, she could stay over once in a while at their place. Or get her own apartment. Why couldn't she put her partner's needs first?

Why? Because Jacinta had goals to achieve. Dreams to fulfill. An obligation to her dead parents to become the best version of herself. She wanted to be a businessman like her boss, Micah Fortune. Why was it that no one ever told a good-looking man he should settle down and have a family? Micah was thirty-four and a determined bachelor. He was handsome and rich enough that he'd have no issues finding a bride, but he didn't want one, saying business came first. As for his looks, describing Micah as handsome was an understatement. Son of Hayden and Darla Fortune, and sister to Vivienne and brother to Drake, his dark blond hair and green eyes reminded Jacinta of young David Beckham, her favorite soccer player besides those currently playing for Chivas of Guadalajara in the Liga MX.

Micah was muscular in that lean, sculpted way those soccer players, or even movie star cowboys, were. If not at the office, Micah could often be found on horseback, going from the boardroom to hands-on with the ranch's cattle with a change of boots. She had no idea why some woman hadn't managed to put a ring on his finger. Jacinta would; that was, if he wasn't her boss, eight years older than her… and, of course, if he wasn't a Fortune.

She wasn't anywhere close to being in his league. While her family was financially stable, next to the Fortunes they were paupers. Then again, almost everyone in Emerald Ridge was when compared to that family. In fact, back in January, when she'd started her internship as his administrative assistant, she'd found Micah intimidating.

However, she'd adjusted and relaxed because Micah was personable, friendly and professional. He treated her with respect and listened to her ideas. Bottom line? She'd won the lottery with her internship.

With a mentor like Micah, she was in the catbird seat. Well, until her grandmother's edict that she get married. Dinner over, Jacinta rose and carried her plate into the kitchen. Then she excused herself to go to her bedroom and sulk. She'd allow herself twenty-four hours for a well-deserved pity party. By tomorrow, if a solution hadn't come to her, she would find one. She would blaze her own path. Her abuela might have forced her hand with her ultimatum, but Jacinta would find a workaround. She would not cave to her grandmother's whims or lose everything she'd worked for.

Micah Fortune knew something was wrong the moment he walked into his office Monday morning. The unsettled vibe wasn't caused by the latest dramas involving his family, troubles he wore like millstones. First, there was the baby his cousin Poppy was fostering after said baby had been left on her doorstep. Then there were the acts of sabotage at area ranches, including his. The thefts and vandalism had caused him many sleepless nights, including this past weekend. His family was no closer to finding the mother of the baby or the saboteur. Bracing himself, he approached his administrative assistant's desk. She was usually a ray of sunshine but today she wore a frown a mile wide. "Good morning, Jacinta."

Her pretty face peered upward. "Good morning, Micah."

He tilted his head at her hollow tone. Did his intern appear tired? Had her smile appeared forced? Something definitely seemed off. "Is everything okay?"

"Of course. It's fine." Jacinta smiled again, but it still didn't reach her eyes. After four months, Micah knew her eyes. He looked into those deep brown orbs daily. Noted the small, light gold flecks scattered across her irises. Felt a strange pull he ignored. Today the brightness had gone, as if someone had turned down the dimmer switch on a light. Had she suffered some sort of bad news?

Concern made him decide the call he needed to make could wait. "Nothing's wrong with your MBA, is it? I've set time aside to look at your business plan. Your professor isn't upset that it's not done yet, is he?"

She shook her head, those long, silky dark strands cascading over her white shirt. He stilled his fingers lest he reach for a wayward piece. "No worries. That's all fine."

He didn't believe her. "You do know that *fine* also means things are frustrating, idiotic, nasty and evolving, right?"

Jacinta's eyes widened. "Those are usually not the words associated with 'fine' when it's being used as an acronym."

Hoping to cheer her up, Micah softened his statement with a grin and light chuckle. "To risk sounding personal, I've never found you insecure, neurotic or emotional. And you're definitely not any of the other things the letter F might stand for."

Jacinta arched a brow. She had Goldilocks brows—not too thick and not to thin. He wasn't a fan of the overplucked look. "You mean I'm not freaked out?"

"*Are* you?" He took the opening and pried. An inner voice insisted he'd do the same for any of his employees. "Nothing bad happened this weekend, did it?"

"A small family issue," Jacinta replied softly. "But nothing that will interfere with my job or my coursework."

He shifted his stance to appear approachable, especially as he was aware of how he towered over her petite figure. He liked Jacinta and wanted her to succeed. "Trust me, I know all about family issues. Tell you what, maybe you can help me with mine and I can help you with yours. We can chat over lunch. We have to discuss your business plan anyway."

"Would you like me to order some food for delivery?"

They often ate lunch in the office, as doing so was efficient. But in this instance, he decided neutral ground would be a better place for her confidences. "Call Francesca's and have them set aside a table. I'd rather not have to wait if there's a tour bus or something."

"I can do that." If she was surprised by his choice to go out, she didn't show it. Even though he'd never taken her there, she knew he often took clients to Francesca's because, unlike the Lone Star Selects steakhouse, which was the most upscale place in town, or Cucina and Captain's, which were located in the Emerald Ridge Hotel, Francesca's Bar and Grill was a family-run, popular lunch and dinner eatery perfect for business luncheon.

"Let's go about twelve thirty." He moved toward his office door but paused. Maybe he should have offered something casual? "Unless you wanted Donatello's Pizza?"

The town pizzeria served single slices of twenty different types of pizza, and had a small, casual dining room for anyone deciding eat in. He preferred something sit-down, but realized belatedly he should have offered her a choice. She might find Francesca's imposing.

"Francesca's sounds perfect. I've never been there."

"Great. You're in for a treat." Micah smiled, something he found himself often doing around her. If she wasn't his intern, he'd have to examine his reactions. As it was, she'd be leaving her position here soon, so no need. "I'll admit to being glad as I've had enough pizza in the last week to tide me over for a year. I'll call you if I need anything. Unless it's family, I'm not available until lunch."

"I'll make sure you're not disturbed."

She would, too, Micah knew. Jacinta was the best assistant he'd ever had. She was smart, funny, personable and a fast learner. His temp had a head for business. Even better, she'd arrived at the right time, as his former administrative assistant had moved out of town with her husband. Expecting human resources to find him a permanent replacement, he'd at first balked when they'd presented him with the idea of mentoring an intern for five months. However, once he'd met Jacinta, he'd signed on. Pushing her attractiveness aside, her eagerness and determination to succeed reminded him of himself at her age. Maybe that's why he took such an interest in her endeavors. In a sense, they were kindred spirits.

Micah had always known what he was going to do for his career, same as Jacinta. He'd run the ranch. She'd make chocolate. Recently, she'd brought him some of Abuela Rosa's chocolate to sample and the candy was exceptional.

Jacinta had both brains and beauty, which made her a force to be reckoned with. The fact that she was so enticing made him even more aware of ensuring he acted in a professional manner. But all of that was a moot point anyway because he'd shut down his heart following a brutal betrayal. Even if something about Jacinta called to his baser urges and desires, he wouldn't act on it. He was done dating and had more important things to worry about, like finding out who was sabotaging the ranch. As the oldest sibling, he felt a strong responsibility to solve the problems, including his plan to go undercover as a ranch hand. He'd get to the bottom of who was causing all the trouble, no matter what it took.

The future of the ranch—and his family—depended on him.

Chapter Two

As Micah opened the door to Francesca's, Jacinta's excitement ran from her head to toes covered in sensible two-inch, black leather pumps. Giddy shivers might not be for business meals, but she had them anyway. She reminded herself to play it cool. After all, she'd made plenty of reservations here for her boss, which explained the warm welcome Micah received when they approached the hostess stand.

"Mr. Fortune, welcome back!" Enthusiasm poured from a midfifties woman with dark hair. "I was delighted when I saw your name. I've saved you the best table."

Micah took her exuberance in stride. "Ah, Francesca, that's kind. And, please, you know it's Micah. I don't stand on ceremony."

The best table, Jacinta noted, was in a raised section that ran the length of the venue. Their two-top was against the railing, meaning Micah sat across from her by design. They had a great view of both the diners below and events occurring outside the large front windows. He held her chair out and his fingers accidentally brushed her back as he pushed her chair in. "Sorry about that."

"No worries." She shifted against the wood to desensitize before unrolling her silverware. Placing her linen napkin in her lap diffused a sudden onset of bubbly nerves.

She'd brushed hands with Micah before. Why this sense of heightened awareness? Reaching for her menu avoided the question, as did studying the venue.

Francesca's relaxed vibe come from its décor of earth tones, stone and wood. Subdued lights provided the perfect amount of illumination. On the floor below, groups of mothers ate alongside their young children, a group of elderly ladies chatted animatedly, and men in neon T-shirts and cargo work pants stretched out after the morning labor. The upper level played host to those in business attire. With ties optional, gentlemen like Micah had undone top buttons and rolled sleeves.

A thirtysomething waiter dressed in all-black approached. "Hello, I'm Elton, and I'll be serving you today. Is this your first time here?"

"It is mine but not his," Jacinta admitted, lowering the menu.

Elton provided two glasses of iced water. "Let me know if I can offer any suggestions. You're in for a treat."

"So he tells me." Jacinta glanced at Micah, noticing he hadn't opened his menu. Her nose wrinkled. "Do you already know what you want?"

A butterfly-inducing grin accompanied a sheepish shrug. "I eat the same thing every time. Elton, give us five so she can browse. I'll take iced tea."

"I'll stay with water," Jacinta said before their server left. The trifold menu contained a dazzling array of mouthwatering choices. "Any suggestions?"

"The burgers are the best in town, as is the chicken spiedini sandwich. But you can't go wrong with anything you choose."

She couldn't resist teasing him. "How would you know? You get the same thing."

A wink made her stomach flip. "Okay, you got me there. But my brother and sister don't order what I get and since they have never complained..." An unabashed tone trailed off before adding, "You should be good with whatever you choose."

Too bad *he* wasn't on the menu. Shocked by the thought, Jacinta nibbled her lower lip and concentrated on the choices.

When their waiter returned, she ordered the chicken spiedini sandwich and substituted a side salad for the French fries. Micah chose the cowboy burger, which was a double patty topped with cheddar, pepper jack, bacon, onion straws and then drizzled with barbecue sauce. Unlike Jacinta, he didn't forgo the fries. He chuckled at her surprised expression. "What? Just because I eat lighter at the office doesn't mean I can't indulge. Today's a splurge. Besides, I run every day. If we order dessert, I'll add another mile."

He'd be the perfect indulgent dessert. Jacinta coughed as a sip of water went down wrong. What had gotten into her?

His brows knit together and he leaned forward. "Are you okay?"

"Hate it when that happens," she managed, patting her lips with the napkin. Somewhat composed, she gave what she hoped passed for a professional smile. Thank goodness he couldn't read her mind. "Shall we chat about my business plan for Abuela Rosa Chocolates?"

That was a far safer topic and, following Micah's, "By all means," she explained what she'd envisioned. "First, I'd like a better location. While the converted garage space meets food safety standards, it's limited to one conveyor line, and that's rarely in use. My grandmother prefers to create everything by hand, which is still possible even if expanded. We could use another line for filled chocolates, like truffles, which is a growth area. Plus, we could also dedicate a line to chocolate-covered confections, such as our caramels. What if both of those were served at your family's guest ranch, for instance? Or we could create small solid chocolates with the Fortune logo."

"I like that idea." Their food had arrived and Micah wiped a drop of barbecue sauce from the corner of his lip. Momentarily distracted, Jacinta refocused. "Truffles have an upscale presence. I've seen recipes that pair specific truffles with specific cocktails. But machinery takes money, as does relocating."

He lifted a fry. "That's what small business loans are for. Do you know how much you'd need?"

"I've included the estimate in my business plan."

His pleased nod warmed her heart. "Great. I've seen pieces as you've written it, but when it's completely finished, I'll review your numbers. That's part of my role as your internship mentor, right?"

"My adviser didn't say it was or wasn't. I wouldn't want to impose." The document had morphed into pages of data.

The wide smile he leveled would bowl over the harshest critic and rolled over any further objection she was harboring. "I'll be happy to do it, Jacinta. You've been a great help over the past few months. Not only have you caught on quickly, but you've been an asset to the company. I'll miss you when you go."

"You've been an excellent teacher," she replied, which was safer than admitting she'd miss him, too, but for reasons besides work.

"I appreciate your vote of confidence in my mentorship abilities," Micah said. "But truthfully, I've been so distracted by deals and family stuff that I don't know how much of a help I've been."

"You've been wonderful." He had.

"You're kind to say that, but I know I haven't been as present as I should have been. My family is dealing with some issues out at the ranch that may require me to be on-site." He locked his gaze on hers. "I might need your help with that because I'll need you to cover for me at the office. I'll explain later."

Jacinta's curiosity rose. As Micah's assistant, she was often privy to confidential information but his tone had seemed more distracted and bothered than usual. Or maybe she'd imagined it, for he was smiling again. "Tell me something else, like are you doing anything fun after graduation? And what have the rest of your classes been like?"

As their conversation shifted, Jacinta relaxed and told him how she'd lived in Dallas during her undergrad days. "I always knew I'd come back to Emerald Ridge, though. It's home and I have family here."

"Same. Living in this town goes beyond tradition. It's…" He struggled for the right word.

"It's a like a calling," Jacinta inserted helpfully. "At least for me. Even if that does make me geographically challenged."

He quirked a brow. "What does that mean?"

"A smaller dating pool. Sorry, I didn't mean to get personal. It's just my grandmother has me frustrated. I'm the bane of her existence."

"She raised you, right?"

"Yes." Jacinta had no idea how to tell Micah about her grandmother's ultimatum. The fact Abuela had made one at all was humiliating and embarrassing. "She swears I'm giving her gray hair."

"I can't believe that. Your evaluation paperwork came by email this morning and I already filled it out. I gave you a perfect score. If you weren't planning on running your grandmother's company, I'd make you a job offer on the spot. You have a solid head for business. Surely she sees that."

Jacinta wished. "Thank you."

"I mean it. You're talented."

Her cheeks heated from his praise. Or maybe it was because he was wiping his lips, which drew her attention to his perfect mouth. That mesmerizing smile once again came her way.

"I like having you around. You've been great at your job and good at keeping me in line. My sister Poppy insists it's an impossible task but somehow you've managed to excel at it." Instead of ketchup, Micah dipped a thick-cut fry in ranch dressing. He slid it between his lips and Jacinta jerked her wayward gaze away. He held out a fry. "Want one?"

"I'm good. But thank you." She pressed her legs together and shifted, the hem of her pencil skirt having climbed to midthigh. Micah's understated sexual aura was lethal. He was hot, *seriously hot*, like an Emerald City sidewalk during a Texas heat wave. She lifted a fork of salad and let the raspberry vinaigrette dance on her tongue. Eating was safe, right?

Or maybe not as a familiar voice called, "Jacinta? Oh, it is you. I thought it was."

A shadow fell over the table and Jacinta gazed upward to face her cousin. "Hello, Sofia."

"At first I couldn't believe that was you." Sofia wore a formfitting, spaghetti-strap, knit minidress and sky-high stilettoes. "I was having lunch with Darci and she was like 'Oh, I think that's Jacinta over there,' and I was like, 'Oh, it can't be because she doesn't date.' Then I remembered Abuela's ultimatum, so I thought you were here trying to land a man by the deadline. Maybe that's why you turned down my help." Sofia left the "Because God knows you probably need it" unspoken.

Jacinta managed to keep the boiling anger contained. "Sofia, this is a business meal. With my *boss*, Micah Fortune."

"Oh." Sofia placed her hand just below her collarbone, emphasizing the lower cut of her dress. "Mr. Fortune. It's so nice to meet you. I'm Sofia Simon. I own The Style Lounge on Emerald Ridge Boulevard."

"Pleasure to meet you," Micah said easily, although Jacinta noted his normal welcoming smile didn't reach his beautiful green eyes.

"We were discussing my business plan," Jacinta said, hoping that would move her cousin along.

Sofia blinked long, doelike lashes. "You mean the one for Abuela Rosa Chocolates?"

"Yes. That one," Jacinta said through gritted teeth.

The woman attempted a sympathetic sigh, which came out far more dramatic than she'd intended. Or perhaps not, Jacinta thought cynically.

"Jacinta, I don't want you to get your hopes up. Abuela is beyond stubborn and there's no way you can make a love match in six weeks." Sofia turned to Micah conspiratorially. "She can't even keep a man past a few dates." She added a quick tsk. "Besides, the chocolate business never makes any money. Selling it would give Abuela time to socialize with her bridge club. She might even think of heading into a retirement village."

"Seventy-five is not *that* old," Jacinta protested. Underneath the table, she twisted the cloth napkin into a tight rope.

"Old enough that she needs guidance. Once I have control, I'm selling everything. You do know a developer is trying to get our double lot so he can turn it into a condo complex, right? Even if he starts with just the garage area, selling will set me—I mean all of us, up for life."

Jacinta's words bit out between clenched teeth. "You can't do that."

Her cousin's serious expression never changed. "But I can and I will. Unless you find a husband by the deadline, and I'm not holding my breath for that." Sofia's phone buzzed and she dug it out of her oversized designer handbag. She glanced at the screen and said, "I've got to take this. Oh, and don't forget to check." She pointed at her mouth and was gone with a backhand wave and an over-the-shoulder, "Adios!"

Jacinta took water and swirled it around to free whatever might be stuck in her teeth.

"Let me see," Micah said.

Embarrassed, Jacinta rolled her lips under. Sofia had deliberately humiliated her.

"Jacinta," Micah coaxed gently. "Trust me." Sighing, she opened her mouth for his perusal. "You're fine. There's nothing there," he assured her. "Who was that? I take it you're related."

"That," Jacinta said, putting emphasis on the first word, "was my cousin Sofia."

"What was she talking about, saying that you have to be married?" He sipped some iced tea. "It sounded ominous."

If the napkin in her lap had been made of paper, Jacinta would have already shredded it. Continuing to twist the white linen, she tried not to get emotional as she explained the entire situation, ending with, "Abuela Rosa Chocolates is my birthright, so to be sidelined…" She blinked but the nightmare lingered.

"Can't you tell your grandmother that your cousin plans to sell to a developer?"

Jacinta wished it were that simple. "Sadly, Abuela won't believe it. Even with you sitting here having heard Sofia, it's my word against hers. I do love my cousin, but there are days that it's hard."

"I can see why," Micah muttered.

To stop clutching the napkin, Jacinta placed both of her hands on the tabletop. "When you were talking about family dramas earlier, I could relate. Hopefully, yours don't include having a grandmother force you to marry." She huffed out a breath. "If I don't, I'll lose everything I've worked for. She's dangling everything I thought would be mine like a brass ring just out of reach. It's emotional blackmail."

Micah reached forward as if to touch her but withdrew his hand before he crossed the line. "I don't understand the 'forcing you to marry' part, but I can also empathize with your frustration and anger. I know those feelings well. If I can't find the person who's stealing from the ranch, my family might lose everything, too."

This was the first time he had mentioned the sabotage, but it wasn't surprising as she knew how tightlipped and private the Fortunes could be. Listening to Micah's problems would be a diversion from her own. She also cared about him, as a boss of course. "What's going on?"

He explained how several ranches in the area had had their fences cut, ending with, "Besides the sabotage, we've personally lost two horses and some pricey saddles."

"That's terrible. Emerald Ridge is such a safe town. It's hard to imagine this is happening."

Micah fisted and released his right hand in quick succession, an indicator of how upset he was. "One of the horses taken was Birdy. My cousin Shane wanted her foals. Says no insurance money can replace her. I hate seeing him this upset." Micah expelled a huge sigh. "We have no clues because the security cameras were disabled. That indicates it might be an inside job, which is a huge problem."

No wonder why Micah had been so distracted lately. "But you said it's other ranches as well."

"That's the part we still don't understand. Courtney Wellington's fence was cut and she lost four head of cattle. My cousins have increased our security but we have acres and acres of pasture. It's hard to monitor it all."

He sipped some more iced tea to calm his frustration. "Worse, now the ranch owners are pointing fingers. Even though we're all being targeted, it's stirred up the past and some long-standing feud between the families that I thought was over. But clearly not."

"Okay, that sounds like worse family drama than mine." Jacinta wanted to comfort him but kept her hands still. "I'm sorry to hear this. Is there anything I can do to help?"

"Unfortunately, no." A shake of his head accompanied another waved fry. "But I appreciate you listening. It's hard to focus because my father keeps reminding me how the other families can't be trusted. To be honest, I'm not sure if any of what's been happening is even related to the feud."

"How did it start?" she asked curiously.

"I don't have all the details but, apparently, the bad blood started over someone stealing someone else's bride or something." He set the fry down and pushed the plate forward. "What I do know is that these thieves are getting around our security. Horse and cattle thefts and the cut fences are bad enough and eating into profits, so the last thing we need is additional strife between the families making things worse."

"Well, you just met Sofia. I might be spilling *her* blood if some developer tears down Abuela's house." Jacinta stabbed her fork into her salad with more force than necessary.

Micah pointed. "Luckily lettuce leaves can't feel anything."

"Not that we know of anyway." She put the bite into her mouth.

Micah reached for his burger, took a bite and washed it down with iced tea. "Thank you again for listening to me vent. I can't tell you how much that means to me to know I can trust you."

"Of course." Pleasure at making his day brighter caused her to smile. "I gave myself twenty-four hours for my pity party. Now that I'm beyond that, I'm trying to focus on controlling the things I can control, not the ones I can't."

"A far better use of your time." The pause lasted a nanosecond before Micah asked, "Why not venture out on your own?"

"What do you mean?" Finished with eating her salad, Jacinta decided to box the second half of her sandwich.

"Forming your own company. If your grandmother won't let you have hers, then you should make your own chocolate. Open your own shop."

Jacinta's forehead creased as her brows knit together. "I'd never thought about that. It almost seems sacrilegious to consider it. Almost a betrayal. Like if you left the Fortune ranch…"

"Point taken."

Once their server returned, Micah paid with the company credit card and they left the restaurant. Micah used two vehicles, the electric crossover model in which they currently rode and a diesel-dually crew cab that could pull a horse trailer and traverse both on and off ranch roads. She'd seen that vehicle in the parking lot once or twice. Large, firm hands turned the steering wheel out of the parking lot, momentarily capturing her gaze before she returned her attention to his handsome profile as he spoke.

"I don't mean to come across as condescending, but I wanted to tell you that I was proud of how you handled Sofia. Not too many people would be able to remain calm. You did well."

"I did stab my salad." Jacinta attempted a smile. "But thanks."

Micah's intensity didn't shift as he navigated the drive to the office. "I'm serious. You've had a huge hiccup in your plans and you didn't rise to her bait. She wanted you to be flustered. I could tell you were ready to explode, but she didn't know."

"I don't think she would have cared one way or another," Jacinta admitted. "She's my cousin. My father and her mother are siblings. Sofia and I didn't grow up in the same household. We aren't that close, more like oil and water."

"How so?"

"Well, in a lot of ways. But careerwise, she was into fashion and I was into cooking. Part of my frustration is that she doesn't have the same connection to Abuela Rosa Chocolate as I do. Abuela raised me. Taught me the recipes."

"That must have been tough losing your parents so young. I'm sorry. I shouldn't have brought that up."

"It's okay. Abuela made sure I had as much love as possible. Minus some memories, she's all I've ever known, all I've had. The debt I owe her is too great for me to ever repay. It's why it hurts that now she wants me married."

Micah pulled into his parking spot and turned off the engine. "That's understandable. Family matters. You care about pleasing her."

"I do. Sofia has no drive to be a chocolatier. The only time she cares about the business is when Abuela gives us our miniscule shares at Christmas. We aren't making money. There's so much potential. Urgh!" Jacinta made two fists and lightly banged them against her thighs. She tugged the skirt down. "All Sofia cares about is taking what she can strip from the place."

"Hey, it'll be okay…" Micah reached to cover Jacinta's hand with his own. As if noticing the same spark of electricity, he removed his hand quickly. "Sorry."

"It's fine." The jolt her boss's touch had given her still pulsed. "It's been a rough weekend. I can't believe I have to marry by the end of May or lose everything to Sofia."

Micah frowned. "I'm surprised your grandmother would choose your cousin over you."

"You don't know my abuela. When she gets something in her head, she becomes the most obstinate, old-school person I know. She wants to see me married with a loving partner by her side as I pursue my big dream."

"Families are complicated. I told you about the drama my uncle Garth just went through, being accused of being Baby Joey's dad by that anonymous text. It turned out it wasn't even true."

Jacinta had been Micah's confidant for that. "I remember. I'm glad that worked out okay. Let's hope for both of our sakes our families' dramas resolve themselves quickly."

"We can agree on that point," Micah said as he held open her car door.

"Thank you for lunch."

"It was my pleasure. You have a graduate seminar now, right?" he asked as they entered the building.

"Yes, with my MBA professor and my classmates. It's

virtual, but it'll take the rest of the afternoon. I'm using one of the conference rooms."

Instead of hopping on the elevator, they ascended the stairs to the second-floor landing. Micah opened the glass doors and trailed her into her office. "Check in with me before you leave for the day."

"I will." Jacinta put her leftovers into the refrigerator and reached for her laptop. She should tell him how grateful she was for listening to her problems with Sofia and Abuela. "Micah, I…"

But he was already gone.

After leaving Jacinta, Micah closed his office door. Unlike the other company offices that had contemporary glass walls and miniblinds, Micah's had drywall and solid doors. His décor was still light and contemporary, a contrast to the traditional rancher stereotypes of heavy wood and Western themes.

He slumped into his ergonomic desk chair, letting the backside hit him when he leaned forward. His and Jacinta's family problems made them quite the pair. Why would her beloved grandmother make such an outrageous ultimatum? Or plan to give her business to Jacinta's unworthy cousin if she failed to marry? Who did that in the twenty-first century? It sounded like the plot of a bad movie.

Speaking of bad movies, the Fortune family had its own dramas, such as the fallout from the anonymous text accusation, which had caused upheaval in Garth and Shelley's thirty-five-year marriage. Every male Fortune had given DNA, and then it had gone missing. Finally, the proof had arrived that Garth wasn't Baby Joey's father. None of the Fortunes was. Having been told once that he, too, was going to be a father had dredged up Micah's own past trauma and caused sleepless nights.

He tapped a finger hard against his desk. Too much drama and thefts were happening. But at least there were some happy endings. His aunt and uncle were back together. His cousins Poppy, Shane and Rafe had found true love. Micah wished he still believed in soulmates, but after the lies and cheating... He stilled his finger. Time to concentrate on making business deals, not love connections.

Except that his capable administrative assistant had to marry in the next few weeks or lose her birthright. His anger boiling on her behalf, he turned his attention to work. Once he'd assured himself that the breed cattle they'd sold to an overseas farm had made it safely onto the cargo plane at Dallas Fort Worth International Airport, Micah mulled over Jacinta's problem, rationalizing that it was a welcome diversion from his own family's strife.

His temporary employee had mentioned that she was going to focus on controlling the things she could control and not the ones she couldn't. He maintained a similar philosophy. No use worrying when he could expend that same energy solving the problem instead. The trick was finding a solution that his moral code could live with. That's why he found himself so annoyed with Jacinta's grandmother. Didn't she know how awesome her granddaughter was? Couldn't she see how Jacinta kept a positive attitude even when faced with adversity? She was *special*, and he was extremely aware of all the positive attributes of his attractive intern. He liked Jacinta a great deal.

Had he met her somewhere else, like on a business trip to Houston or Dallas, he might have asked her out or considered a brief affair. He closed his eyes momentarily, picturing Jacinta. Her long hair shimmered against her midback.

And her bottom lip? It was full and plump, making her mouth one that a man not only wanted to kiss but to also draw that lower lip between his own. And her long neck would be perfect for tracing with the backs of his fingers until he stroked her collarbones.

Micah went to the minifridge hidden behind a panel and withdrew a bottle of water. He uncapped and swallowed half the contents in one giant gulp, the chilled liquid doing little to quench his parched throat or divert his illicit thoughts. Since her arrival in January, he'd prided himself on his professionalism, minus reaching for her hand today in the car. He still couldn't believe he'd made that lapse in judgment. Touching her had lit a fire, made that devil on his shoulder taunt him that soon she'd no longer be working for him.

He downed the rest of the water and tightened his grip on the empty bottle. The sound of crumpling plastic summed up his conflicting feelings nicely. He had to crush them.

Even after she no longer worked for him, thinking of her in any other way than as a coworker he'd once known would be inappropriate. She was also too young. She should date someone far less jaded and world-weary. Twenty-six was the time in a person's life when they had the world at their feet, and Jacinta was no different. She deserved to follow her dreams and have her own company, whether that be her grandmother's or something new.

Micah returned to his desk as an idea took hold. As a CEO with a buck-stops-here attitude, he was the one ultimately responsible for the Fortunes' cattle, the workers who oversaw them and the operation's upkeep. But that didn't mean he didn't have other interests. He was a silent investor in several ranches in the area, along with several small businesses in Emerald Ridge, such as Francesca's.

He preferred to keep his involvement to a minimum, stepping in only if he saw a problem. Having a successful town where people wanted to live meant his family could attract the best people to work for the ranch. As he profited, he reinvested. Because of this he'd grown even wealthier, but so had the town, which was now one of the richest in the state. Everyone had benefitted.

Drake and Rafe had their own version of giving back with their Gift of Fortune mission, a joint goodwill initiative to send invitations for a stay at the Fortune's Gold Ranch to those who were in need of an escape. Nominations came through an online form. His brother and cousin figured that a stay at an exclusive, luxe guest ranch and spa was a good way to help people heal, to help them get over a broken heart or allow them to work on a rocky marriage.

And the positive PR hadn't hurt either.

Micah knew no amount of spa therapy would heal his own scars, but he was a lost cause anyway. However, Janita *wasn't*. He wanted to help her, and as a plan began to form, he realized investing in her dream would be no different from helping any of the other townsfolk. It was the least he could do. He reached for his desk phone and pressed the intercom button. "Jacinta, will you come in here?"

She rapped on the door before she entered, her professional smile warm and friendly. "What can I do for you?"

Everything. He drank her in as she entered, her white silk shirt forming a tantalizing yet office appropriate V. The black pencil skirt skimmed her knees, and the practical pumps she wore failed to lessen his giantlike height. She tilted her head as she waited his instructions, the long hair swishing against her shoulders. After a quick mental shake, he focused on the matter at hand—*business*—not her beauty.

"I'd like to visit the chocolate factory. It'll help me give you better feedback on your business plan. Will that work?"

Her forehead creased, creating a shallow river his finger itched to smooth. "It's a converted two-car garage."

"Still, it will help me understand your plans if I can see how the place operates. I don't even know if you make chocolate daily, or what making it by hand means. Will you ask your grandmother if a visit would be acceptable? She wants you to pass your course, right? She'll at least do that much for you, won't she?"

"I would think so." Unconsciously, Jacinta nibbled on her bottom lip, making it even fuller. "We finished most of the orders this weekend, but there are leftovers that have to go out this Thursday. Once we finish those, she'll take a break for Easter."

"Then I should see the operation as soon as possible. I would assume your expansion plan includes making chocolate on a daily basis."

How had he never noticed that the ends of her hair danced when she nodded? "Yes, unless we're shutting the conveyor belt down for cleaning, which has to be done when we switch candy types, my goal would be increase the operation to daily. My grandmother can be temperamental in her work habits."

"A very politically correct way of putting it."

Jacinta arched one of her perfect brows. "You said it, I didn't."

He laughed. "I did and I'll own it. Developing a corporate calendar is important in any business, as is ensuring that your employees will be present when you need them on the job. Since you know my schedule, why don't you reach out to your grandmother and find out when I can come by this week? The sooner, the better."

"I'll see what I can do."

Jacinta nibbled her lip again and Micah averted his gaze lest he wonder yet again what it would be like to kiss her. He coughed. "I'll leave you to it then. Again, set me to 'do not disturb' unless it's family. I've got some proposals on my desk and I want to give them my undivided attention."

He also needed to get her lips and visions of kissing her out of mind.

When she turned, he got a great view of her backside and the shiny black hair that cascaded halfway down. He sank into his desk chair, proud of his self-control and the fact he'd stayed on the other side of his desk and not moved closer as if drawn in like a moth to the porch light. He'd been nothing but professional. Disturbed by his lustful thoughts but satisfied by his decorum, Micah returned to work.

Chapter Three

One thing Jacinta had learned early—putting on a hairnet was awkward. Donning one while standing before Micah? Doubly awkward. There was no art to hairnet placement and often the net went everywhere first.

Today, Jacinta had worn her hair in a ponytail, so she'd started from the front, with the net covering her forehead. Then she'd lifted her hair and slid the net around. Finally, she'd tucked any wayward strands under the elastic that cut into her forehead until she pushed it higher on her head.

"You'd think I'd be better at this," Micah complained. His dark blond hair stuck out in several spots and he jabbed the offending locks with his fingertips. It was Thursday afternoon and they stood underneath the awning outside the 24-by-24-foot, two-car garage that served as the home of Abuela Rosa Chocolates. The rain had luckily held off. Micah's fingers fumbled as the hairnet shifted.

"Here, let me," Jacinta said. Even with a low heel, she gazed up at him. "Do you mind?"

"No. Please." He leaned forward and bent his head. Jacinta rose on tiptoe and lifted the hairnet so she could push the loose strands into place. Her breath hitched as her fingertips ran over his hairline and the back of his neck. "There. Got you covered."

He straightened and, if she didn't know better, she would have sworn his light green eyes had darkened to jade. "Good. Don't want to spoil the chocolate."

He couldn't spoil anything, Jacinta thought. Her grandmother was going to love him as much as she did, as a boss of course. When she had told her grandmother that Micah had asked to see the "factory," Abuela had immediately agreed, most likely due in some part to the power of the Fortune name. Jacinta prayed his visit would loosen her grandmother's resolve of making her marry in order to take over the business. Hairnets in place, Jacinta rang the bell.

The heavy steel door opened and Abuela stood there, her white apron dotted with splotched chocolate. Her own hairnet-covered head lifted so she could meet Micah's gaze. "Mr. Fortune," she said. "I'm Rosa Gomez."

"Call me Micah." He followed her inside, Jacinta on his heels as the door shut behind them. They stopped about six feet inside the room, with her boss immediately filling it with his magnetic presence.

Micah gave her grandmother a warm smile. "Jacinta has told me wonderful things about your chocolate. Says she learned everything from you."

"She still has many things to learn," Abuela retorted.

Jacinta was glad he couldn't see her wince. Micah, to his credit, didn't miss a beat. "You know what they say, if you're green, you're growing and if you're ripe, you rot. I hope I'm always a lifelong learner. If not, what's the point?"

Nice save, Jacinta thought, Micah's stock rising further in her estimation. Abuela tilted her head and studied him, but while her grandmother's eyes narrowed, she said nothing.

"What are you making today?" Jacinta asked, trying to shift the dynamic.

"We shipped the last of the molded chocolate earlier this week. Today we're making the perishables, the chocolate-covered marshmallows and the chocolate-covered strawberries. Those orders will be delivered tonight and then we'll shut down for Easter. I don't work on Good Friday or next week."

"You won't hear me complain," Micah said easily. "The boss makes the rules."

"Absolutely." Upon saying this, Abuela caught Jacinta's gaze, as if to wonder if Micah was for real. Jacinta held her lips tight and managed not to frown. Her grandmother was being slightly cantankerous today.

One bright side was at least that Micah would see what she was up against. He would also ascertain what Jacinta had to work with, and why the business needed to be expanded. She hovered in the background and listened as Abuela showed him around the 576-square-foot space. She showed him the kitchen area where she made her own caramel using copper kettles that she filled with pure cane sugar, fresh whipping cream, butter and Mexican vanilla "Once molded and set, I then cut them and dip them in chocolate and sprinkle them with sea salt."

Today the kettles were empty and coated marshmallows were chilling, so Abuela focused on the strawberries. "I must make the chocolate first," she said. "I make big batches, melting down the bars to use as I need them." She pointed to smooth, liquid-like chocolate that was gently spinning in a tempering machine.

"Since we have many orders, today I am using the belt. You'll see I've poured the chocolate in here." She showed Micah where it went into the machine and he watched as the machine covered each strawberry with the liquefied chocolate. Then, as the strawberries moved onward, the next part of the conveyor belt shook off the excess covering. Before the chocolate-covered berries reached the chiller, one of her grandmother's part-time workers used a squeeze bottle to paint on a squiggly white stripe. "No matter what, we always finish by hand," Abuela boasted. "These are handcrafted."

"When did you first get this machine?" Micah asked.

"*Mi amado esposo*—my beloved husband—found it when a factory in Dallas shut down. We could not afford it, and I told him I didn't need it, but he insisted. He was always doing things like that."

"The investment paid off then, as you're using it to fulfill your Easter orders," he noted. "Do you track your sales? Look at where you might have been able to do more?"

"More is not always better," Abuela said. "Sometimes more is simply more work."

"True," Micah acknowledged. He glanced over Abuela's head and caught Jacinta's gaze before returning focus to her grandmother. "What is your favorite type of chocolate to make?"

"A rose tea chocolate. I infuse tea in the chocolate and sprinkle actual dried rose petals onto the top of the chocolate as it cools."

"Rose petals are edible?" Micah appeared shocked. "Truly?"

Abuela appeared pleased by his surprise. "Yes. I have some rose tea chocolate bars in the house." She turned to Jacinta, as if noticing her for the first time. "Why don't you go inside and grab a bar of chocolate for Mr. Fortune?"

"*Micah,*" he insisted.

Abuela didn't acknowledge his correction. Instead, her focus remained on her granddaughter and the warning Jacinta read in her gaze. "Besides, it'll give us time to talk, CEO to CEO."

* * *

Micah tracked Jacinta as she left the garage. Before the door closed, he could see her yank off her hairnet, as if agitated. His first instinct was to go after her, but he checked his reaction as Rosa began explaining how she boxed the chocolates. Anywhere from three to twelve strawberries went into plain white boxes and then a gold-metallic stretch string was looped around the box before being tied into a bow that would hold the lid tight. "You don't print on your packaging?"

A brown-eyed gaze similar to Jacinta's held his without blinking. "Why? Printing costs money and people throw the box away. Those who buy my chocolate know where it comes from."

"Yes, but it's a subtle way of reminding them of your brand. We use FGR on everything from towels to napkins to stationery at the guest ranch. It adds an elevated, personal touch."

"Your operation is far bigger than mine," Rosa stated. "And I don't have a similar need or desire. I like things simple, Mr. Fortune. People want the chocolate, not the wrapper."

Seeing she wasn't going to call him Micah, he didn't bother correcting her again. "But what if production could remain simple yet better? I'm impressed with the quality of the chocolate you produce, even more so after I've seen how it's made. My cousin Poppy is always looking for local vendors to showcase at the ranch and spa. We could serve them at Fortune's Gold. Bring you even more business."

For a tiny woman, she had an oversized presence as she stared at him. "Is this in Jacinta's business plan? Because while my granddaughter is brilliant in her way, she doesn't understand that enlarging the company means losing quality. She won't believe that I'm satisfied with how things are. I know this crushes Jacinta, but my granddaughter doesn't understand as she's not old enough to do so. She does not have the life experience that I have. That even you have."

A dig about his age could slide, but Micah couldn't let his employee be disparaged. "But isn't that how we grow? Even at thirty-four, I'm still learning. I still make mistakes. How can I fulfill my destiny if I'm not allowed the opportunity to succeed? Or to fall flat on my face, if that's what it takes first. Henry Ford's first two attempts at commercial automobile production were failures, but then he revolutionized the industry with the Model A."

Rosa's arms folded across the chocolate-covered apron. "But I do not want to be Henry Ford, even if half of the trucks on Texas roads are made by the company that bears his name."

"Your granddaughter is one of the best administrative assistants I have ever had the opportunity to work with. She has a head for business. I'd find her a place in one of my family's companies in a heartbeat but she desires to honor your legacy. I've read most of her business plan, and it's sound. I wouldn't be so willing to help her pursue her dream if not."

She studied him as if trying to decide if he was telling the truth or being swayed by a pretty face. In the end, Rosa dug in without choosing, her obstinacy evident. "Yes, but it's not what I want for her, and as it is *my* company. That's a lesson she'll have to learn."

Micah could see that Rosa meant what she said, and he didn't know if Jacinta had told her grandmother that he knew that Rosa's business would go to her cousin Sofia unless Jacinta got married. He recognized he'd pushed the older woman as far as he could without bringing offense, which was why he didn't warn her that she might risk alienating her granddaughter forever if she held fast to her ultimatum.

A buzz sounded and Micah followed Rosa to the door. "Thank you so much for the tour," he said before stepping out into the cloudy day and removing the hairnet. He placed it in the nearby covered trashcan.

"I have the chocolate," Jacinta told her grandmother. She held out a small sandwich-sized bag.

"That's for Mr. Fortune," Rosa said. "I'll see you when you get home later. Thank you both for dropping by."

The door closed in his face with a definitive click.

Micah rounded the back of his car and opened the passenger door for Jacinta. As she climbed in, a big fat raindrop hit his face. A glance at the sky revealed that the gray clouds had knit together. More drops fell.

He slid inside, strapped in and started the engine. The car made no noise as it moved forward. "I see what you meant. She's stubborn. You're one hundred percent right about that."

Jacinta sighed. "Abuela's convinced she's right. She believes she's doing the best thing for me. Be married. Be happy. When that's not what I want."

He hated her resignation. "We'll have to find a way to convince her otherwise."

Micah's phone buzzed and he glanced at the infotainment system as the computer voice read the notification. "Do you mind if we stop by the ranch? That's the package I've been waiting for."

"Sure, you're the boss."

Micah grinned. "That I am, so let's take a detour. Maybe we'll come up with a plan to convince your grandmother along the way."

* * *

Located five miles from downtown, Jacinta had driven by parts of the three-thousand acre Fortune's Gold Ranch before, but she'd never had a reason to enter the property. She certainly couldn't afford to stay there, unlike her favorite singer Taylor Swift, who had visited, if the rumors were true. The ranch had several gates and entrances, but the fanciest were the wrought-iron ones that denoted the main entrance to the guest ranch portion of the property.

Micah drove through that gate but instead of continuing straight, he turned onto a side road and headed toward a smaller building. "These are the ranch offices. Let me go grab what was delivered."

"You didn't have it sent to your house?"

"You'll see why later. I'll be right back." Micah darted in and out of the office. He pointed the crossover in a different direction and soon they passed a series of houses set apart from each other. Jacinta craned her neck. Abuela had a decent-sized house, but these dwarfed hers. "Is this some sort of subdivision?"

"You could say that. That's Poppy's. That's Shane's." He continued to narrate as they drove past the rest of the houses. "And this is mine." Micah parked the car at a white-stucco, two-story house with wood accents. A steep roofline gave an appearance of added height. "This is why it's easier to send things to the ranch office. Much more central for the delivery drivers." He opened his door and came to open hers. "Come inside so that I can put this away."

"The exterior is lovely." Jacinta meant it. One thing she'd loved as a little girl was seeing all the big Texas houses and dreaming that one day she'd have one of those. When she'd mentioned it once to Abuela, her grandmother had told her that a bigger house meant more to clean. Jacinta doubted a man of Micah's stature cleaned his own house.

"All the houses are miniature variations of the main house, which is shared by my father and his cousin, my uncle Garth. We'll drive by that on the way out. You can see where I grew up."

Having seen pictures of the Fortune mansion, which Garth and Hayden Fortune and their wives lived in, Jacinta knew the manse would be even bigger and more impressive in real life, given that Micah's large house was a mini version. She stepped out on the aggregate driveway and then made her way onto a front walk made of wide, custom pavers closely knit together. Even the landscaping was exquisite, showcasing the blooming white and bright blue flowers.

She waited on the front porch while Micah unlocked the oversized wood-stained door. The bright entry foyer rose two stories, and a curved staircase led upward. Because of the open railing, she could see the house had two separate wings that were separated by the walkway at the top of the stairs. "Wow," she said, lowering her gaze to the great room, where the ceilings were two stories as well. A wall of windows let in an expansive view of the fields beyond the fenced portion of the yard. The ranch was so big, she couldn't see the cattle. "Where are they?"

"The breeding ranch is at the far end of the ranch property, away from the guest ranch and spa," he said. "There are small cabins in that area for ranch hands, and a few barns where several horses are kept. There's also riding stables and corrals."

"I'm impressed and a bit overwhelmed by the entire operation and the fact that you live here."

Balancing the cardboard shipping box under one arm,

Micah punched a code into his phone and the beeping of the security system ceased. "I know. This is something, isn't it? My mom designed it. Each of us got a house on our twenty-first birthday, not that mine was ready until I was out of college. This place is intimidating, even for me. I have rooms I haven't seen for months. It's not like I entertain here either."

All Jacinta had gotten for college graduation was a congratulatory card from her grandmother, a cake and another reminder from the university that she had an installment due on her tuition payment plan. Her twenty-first birthday had been drinks with Kim, Katie and Carolyn, after a celebratory dinner with the family.

She followed Micah into a kitchen three times the size of Abuela's. The island was at least ten feet long and six feet deep. The cherry cabinets were forty-two inches and topped with crown molding. While her grandmother had newer appliances, they weren't the higher end ones that Jacinta recognized from watching that home channel show about lottery dream homes. Not that she watched that channel regularly, but Sofia kept it on at the hair salon. Micah set the cardboard box down, reached into his pants pocket and withdrew a Swiss Army knife. He sliced into the tape on top and began to remove the contents.

"Why do you have a wig?" Jacinta asked as he withdrew fake black hair from a plastic bag.

He shook out the strands. "I'm going undercover on the ranch. It's the best way to find out what's happening and who might be sabotaging us. We've haven't located the person who's stealing but we know it has to be someone on the inside, or at least someone who has insider information. The best way for me to ferret out the thief or the mole is to work alongside them. They won't tell their secrets to me as the CEO, but you'd be amazed how people talk when they think you're one of them."

Jacinta grew concerned. "But that could be dangerous. You could be hurt."

Micah's wry smile did nothing to reassure her. "So could any of the men loyal to me. I'm CEO, but I grew up learning how to ride, rope and wrangle. I wouldn't ask my men to do anything I wouldn't do myself. Ranching is hard work, and just because I sit in an office most days doesn't mean I won't get my hands dirty. No soft hands here." He set the wig aside and showed her his palms.

"No," Jacinta agreed. He had lovely hands, hands that would caress a woman tenderly, giving her the delight of fingertips that were rough yet smooth. Hard yet gentle. One hundred percent sensational. She gave a small shiver and wondered if the air-conditioning had kicked on.

Micah opened a cabinet and grabbed two tall glasses. He filled them with ice and water before handing her one. "The weather's been crazy lately. Need to stay hydrated."

"Thanks." Trying not to watch the way his throat moved as he drank, she took a long sip. Micah was as majestic as the house in which she stood. Seeing this side of him reinforced what she knew from the office, that everything about Micah screamed honor and decency. He planned to go undercover because he was hands-on and determined to do what was right. That got her thinking of his hands again, a dangerous path to tread. Micah was her boss. Her *very rich* boss. She'd known he was wealthy, but after seeing the ranch and his house, he was next-level rich.

Micah drained his water and put the glass in the dishwasher. "You know, after meeting with your grandmother today, I think I might have a solution."

"What? You've found me an acceptable husband?" Jacinta set her glass on the granite counter. "Sorry, that was uncalled for."

"Don't apologize. One rule of business, if a man wouldn't apologize for something, then a woman shouldn't either. Your sarcasm didn't offend me. She's put you in an impossible situation and, after meeting your cousin, I can understand why you're so upset. Sofia may own a salon, but she doesn't have the same passion for the chocolate business as you do, not if she wants to sell and bulldoze everything." Using his first two fingers, he tugged on his lower lip. "This is what you've dreamed of, what you've worked for, not Sofia."

"All true." He'd listened to her, understood why Jacinta had hustled so hard to have little undergraduate student loan debt. In her business plan, she'd worked her MBA debt amount into her salary as a full-time employee and owner of Abuela Rosa Chocolates. "It's all I've wanted," Jacinta agreed. "Unfair sure, but it *is* my grandmother's company to do as she sees fit."

"Which is why you should buy it. Not have her give it to you. Offer her money and have her sell to you."

Jacinta tried not to laugh, or cry, or whatever the conflicting emotions rushing through her. What money? Unlike Micah, she didn't come from wealth or have appliances that cost the same as a car—her gaze lighted on something outside—or an in-ground pool that cost more to install than the current value of her grandmother's house. She brought the water to her lips and found herself grateful she got a sip down without choking.

"I can see you're a bit shocked," Micah said. "But I'm a silent investor in multiple ventures around the town. I'm offering you up to two hundred thousand to buy the business outright from your grandmother."

This time she *did* sputter. What would it be like to have those kinds of funds? "Two hundred thousand?" The words came out between small coughs and she took another sip of water.

"Are you okay?" When she nodded, he continued. "The business is probably not worth that much. Start at one hundred thousand, but I'll go up to three hundred if an appraisal says it's worth that. The equipment in the garage is old and your expansion plan calls for a warehouse. That means you wouldn't knock down the house and garage for condos, which should make your grandmother happy." Clearing his throat, he said, "I doubt she wants developers to remove her from her home. I can help you find a suitable location. The money from the sale would allow her to fix whatever's needed to keep her house."

Jacinta managed to find her voice. "You saw how stubborn my grandmother is. She's not going to agree to this."

"Then use the money to buy out Sofia. From my initial impressions, I'm sure she'll jump at the possibility to put cash in her pocket."

"She has seemed like something's going on lately, but I don't know what. And your offer is generous." Jacinta was awed by his gesture. "Why are you doing this?"

Micah's shoulders lifted before dropping. "Because I read the draft of the business plan you gave me and it's solid. Because in addition to being the CEO of the livestock operation of this ranch, that's what I do. I invest. You, Jacinta, are worth the investment."

His forceful, declarative words sent a raw thrill rushing through her. She was worth the investment to a man like Micah, who'd won the lottery with his looks and business acumen? Heat bloomed and spread at the notion. "Thanks."

"You're welcome. I'm your mentor, and I can continue

to act in that capacity. There's some legalities to take care of as we'd want a formal agreement as to how our partnership would look and work, but that's nothing I haven't done before with other proprietors." His green eyes locked on hers. "If you're nervous, I can give you the names of several businesses that I'm partnered with and you can speak with the owners. You met Francesca today. I'm a silent partner in her place."

No wonder why she'd greeted him so warmly. For a brief moment, Jacinta let herself imagine the possibilities. She'd own Abuela Rosa Chocolates. Her business plan would work. Micah would be an investor, so instead of a bank loan, she'd have a private one. A jolt of satisfaction powered an excitement she hadn't felt in a while. And he'd continue to be her mentor. The gorgeous Micah, working one-on-one with her to make her dreams of being a chocolatier come true. Micah and chocolate? If she could pull it off, it was win-win.

Chapter Four

After Micah's offer, Jacinta floated on the proverbial cloud nine until reality intruded and crashed her down. "I'm flattered," she told Micah after the giddiness of his investment offer dissipated. "I'm honored by your faith in me. I can't tell you what this means, or what an ego boost it is."

"You sound like you're about to say no."

Jacinta set her water glass on the granite island. "I'm not the one who will turn it down. I plan to ask, but I already know the answer from both Abuela and Sofia will be no."

When he shook his head more savagely than necessary, the dark blond strands fell onto this forehead. He pushed them back. "I can't believe they would reject your offer, reject *you*. I wish they saw what I do, the potential you have."

His words were a balm to her battered soul and Jacinta would remember them always. "My grandmother wants me married, Micah. She was wed at a young age and had my father, et cetera, et cetera. She's using my dream against me. As for Sofia, am I petty for saying that I think she's always been a little jealous? That she was a bit of a mean girl to me while we were growing up? I was the awkward geeky one to her sophistication."

Micah shook his head again but said nothing.

"Sofia won't mind seeing me lose what I love. She believes that I'm the favorite, even though I don't think that's true. It's just that when my parents died, Abuela took me in and raised me. That doesn't mean that my grandmother loves Sofia less, but my cousin didn't live with Abuela, so perhaps her perspective is skewed."

Micah lifted the wig. "And I thought *my* family was complicated. But they don't sabotage their own kin."

"That's how it's been my entire life," Jacinta said with a heavy sigh. "As for selling, there have been previous attempts to buy my grandmother out. She's refused each time. She will never sell the business to anyone but family. The recipes are generational secrets. While I know them, I can't steal her trade secrets and use them in my own company."

"No, you can't do that," Micah agreed.

"Which is why your proposal is a great idea but impossible. To expand, I can take her existing recipes and modify them. However, I don't have the talent to develop my own recipes, even if I had the time. It's more than simply swapping out the cocoa beans." She paced slightly as a fact dawned. "If you don't mind, I might be taking you up on that offer to help me to find a job though."

Micah didn't disappoint by backing out. Instead, he reinforced his promise. "I meant what I said. I will find a position somewhere in the Fortune family of companies that's worthy of your talents and your degree. I don't want to see your abilities wasted."

He was the best of men. "That's kind." More than. His offer had touched her. Had anyone believed in her like this before? As she became emotional, he stepped toward her.

The ringing of the doorbell interrupted and Jacinta stepped backward quickly and tried to calm a heart racing faster than it should. She prayed her face hadn't flushed as the thumping grew closer and a deep-voiced "Hello!"

echoed off the great room walls. A tall man wearing jeans, boots and a long-sleeved plaid shirt stepped into view. His eyes widened when he saw them. "Oh, sorry, Micah. I didn't realize you had company."

"No, it's fine. Jacinta, you've met my cousin Shane before, right? He runs the guest ranch stables. Shane, this is Jacinta, my administrative assistant intern."

"I've seen you once or twice at the office. Nice to meet you again," Shane said, shaking her hand. Unlike Micah's touch, his didn't give her any tingles. She noted Shane's hair was darker than his cousin's and his eyes blue instead of green. "Sorry to drop in, but I saw your car."

"Any news?" Micah asked as Shane grabbed a glass. "I've got the wig here. A few more pieces left to be delivered and I'll be ready."

Shane pressed the glass against the water dispenser. "Let's hope we get to the bottom of the issue before you wearing a disguise is necessary."

"How about I leave you two to talk for a minute?" Jacinta said. "Do you mind if I go outside?"

Without waiting for an answer, she slid through the French doors off the breakfast room. The day's heat hit her as she stepped out onto the covered back porch that ran the entire width of this wing of the house. Micah had an outdoor kitchen with a built-in grill and pizza oven. There were tables and chairs sitting on a floor made of the same wide pavers as the front walkway. She perched on one section of the L-shaped couch. Along with the matching love seat, the furniture faced an outdoor fireplace with a large, mounted TV above the mantel. Ceiling fans created a gentle breeze. Her neck swiveled as she absorbed the wealth in her surroundings. The pool's rocky waterfall feature gurgled and a fountain created a gentle spray.

"Sorry about that," Micah said a few minutes later as he closed the door behind him. He sat near her.

She gestured. "This is beautiful out here."

"If you had your suit, I'd say we should go for a swim. I'm not in that pool enough besides to do laps, but at least I get to look at it."

What would it be like to live like this? "I think I'd be in it every day. I love to swim. In college, my exercise was swimming endless laps."

"Well, how about I give you a gate code and you can drop by anytime and use it. You know my schedule and I'm almost never here. In fact, you could house-sit for me when I'm undercover. Keep the lights on. Make people think I'm around. But we can talk about that later," he added hurriedly.

"How's Shane handling the theft of his horse?" Jacinta's pet had passed once and she'd been devastated. She couldn't imagine having an animal stolen by someone. She'd fight tooth and nail to get a beloved pet back.

Micah fingered the wicker. "Not well, but better now that he just got engaged to Naomi Katz. She's an image consultant and she's good for him."

"I've never met her but her grandmother is a long-time customer of ours. It's a sweet story. Her husband used to buy her Abuela's chocolate every year for her birthday, but one year her birthday fell on Passover and he couldn't buy them for her."

Micah settled deeper onto the couch opposite her. Light rain began to fall again, the droplets making ripples on the pool surface. Safe under the protective cover of the porch, the noise was soothing. "Why couldn't she buy any? Your grandmother sells chocolate if it's ordered, right?"

"Yes, but for those celebrating Passover, part of the ritual is eating foods that are prepared a special way and avoiding others. Anyway, my grandmother made Naomi's grandmother this special Passover chocolate so she could still have her birthday tradition. Now, every year at Passover, she makes them a small amount to continue the new tradition."

"I didn't know there was such a thing as Passover chocolate, and the fact you know that amazes me. All the more reason to expand." He turned toward her, his eyes glimmering. "I know that your grandmother thinks she's helping by forcing you to marry, but family is what you make of it. Look at my cousin Poppy. She's fostering a baby that's not hers. She's had Joey from when he was one day old. If the mother isn't found, I expect her to petition to adopt, and her fiancé is on board. Do you know Leo Leonetti? He co-owns the century-old vineyards with his three sisters?"

Jacinta redid her ponytail. "Can't say I run in those circles, so no."

"He's my age, anyway, so unless you'd bumped into him, it makes sense you wouldn't have met. He and my cousin used to date, and now they're engaged."

"You seem almost surprised by that."

"In a way I am. All three of my cousins are now engaged. At the start of the year we were all single, and now each one of Uncle Garth's kids is headed for the altar."

"Sadly, I don't have any ex-boyfriend who can save me from my predicament." Jacinta tried to temper her frustration. Everyone else could find someone, and she was the one with the ticking clock who needed a fiancé the most. "I'm not dating anyone, so there's no way I'm getting married in a month. I couldn't even order a mail-order-groom that fast, or get on by doing one of those married-at-first-sight shows." She gave a small shudder. "As if."

Micah picked at some lint on his slacks. "That makes me glad. You should marry for love. You deserve to have it all."

"Can I though? It's frustrating to be forced to find a man. This is the twenty-first century, for heaven's sake. Women do *not* need to be married. Neither do men. But my abuela doesn't agree."

Micah held up his hands in mock surrender. "You'll get no argument from me on any of those points. What is it about people who are in relationships anyway?" he scoffed. "Why do they feel the need to matchmake? The rest of us do not need or want their help."

"Exactly. It's so annoying." Jacinta couldn't believe how in sync they were on this topic. "I'd like to be established in my career first. Why can't they understand that?"

"I am established in my career, and everyone is still trying to fix me up," he muttered darkly. "I was in a long-term relationship that ended last year, and let's say that once bitten equals twice shy. I have no plans to ever give my heart away again, thanks to her lying and cheating."

She winced. "Ouch. I'm sorry."

"I've moved past it, but I won't forget it. Lesson learned. I do not plan on involving my heart ever again. I'm too busy with work anyway. You've seen me."

"You put in more hours than anyone I've ever seen." He did. He led by example.

"That's what bosses should do. I can't expect one hundred percent from my staff if I don't give the same. The woman I was with didn't understand that, and well, let's just say that finding her the way I did wasn't what I expected. There's more to the story, but it's not worth mentioning."

Jacinta could imagine what had happened. "She should have been honest with you, especially if her feelings had changed. She shouldn't have kept stringing you along."

"Agreed. But turns out her main interest was the fortune that accompanies my last name."

Jacinta face scrunched. "I dislike people like that. It's dishonest. My bad-boyfriend story pales in comparison, but one of my exes told me he didn't think I would amount to much."

Micah leaned forward. "What a complete idiot. If I saw him those would be fighting words. You are so talented. I've already told you that. If I sing your praises more, it could be suspect."

His compliments fed her ego. "Yeah, which honestly helps me heal because I'll admit his words wounded. What made the situation worse was that it happened in front of at least twenty other people. I'm not sure if they were simply shocked or if they agreed, but no one defended me. Not one person told him that the vile things he spewed made him look like a terrible person. That night I discovered who my real friends were, and it wasn't anyone at that party. I called for a ride and went home."

"I hope you never saw that bastard again."

She liked how Micah defended her, could get used to it if she wasn't careful. As the breeze picked up, her ponytail swished. She removed the holder and let the strands fall loose before securing her hair. "I had a class with him and there were two weeks left. But I didn't speak to him and didn't hang out with those people. One of my true friends, who worked for the professor as a teacher's assistant the next semester, later told me I'd gotten the highest grade in the class and that he'd only gotten a C. The professor used my paper as an example of one of the best he'd seen."

"There you go," Micah said. "There's some satisfaction in that." Suddenly, he tensed. "He doesn't work for me, does he?"

She shook her head. "Oh no, this was back in undergrad school. He's in Louisiana now. I'll admit to having done a little LinkedIn stalking. You don't have interests in Shreveport, do you?"

"No. Would you like me to?"

She laughed, unsure if Micah was serious. "No, I'm good. He's like midlevel manager or something. Your company is safe."

"That's good because I'd fire him for being a jerk to you, no matter how good of an employee he was. My memory is long."

She couldn't tell if Micah was joking, and she was afraid to ask. They sat on porch, the world a blur because of the gentle rain.

"You deserve the best, Jacinta. You know that saying. 'You get what you want and then you get what you deserve.' That idiot got what he wanted, which was to humiliate you, and now he's going to get what he deserves, which is to be a midlevel manager his whole life. You will be a CEO."

"That's the dream." She took a final sip of water.

His sincere gaze held hers, green eyes to brown. "It's not a dream. It's reality. I might not be psychic, but I can predict your future with absolute certainty. Don't despair, because even if you lose Abuela Rosa Chocolates, there's something else even better coming along. I know it."

His faith in her overwhelmed. When a man like Micah spoke, people listened. She'd lucked out to land him as her mentor, and in a sense, a friend. "Curiosity, and you don't have to answer. Did she get what she deserved? The one who hurt you?"

"*Betrayed* me is a better word for her actions. Hurt assumes that I still have feelings other than bitterness. She wounded my pride, and honestly, I don't know where she is. She moved to Amarillo with the guy she cheated on me with. Some sort of fitness instructor or something, and yes, I know that's so cliché. But she didn't marry a Fortune, so in a way she did lose out. This—" he gestured "—is not hers."

And for some reason she didn't want to consider, Jacinta was extremely glad. Oh, not about the fact that Micah had been burned, but because he was single and not stuck with some gold digger, a woman who'd cheated, who'd wanted him because of his money. Infidelity and gold-digging would damage anyone's psyche, and she hoped Micah would eventually find a real love match.

At least she'd never endured that specific humiliation, or if she had, she remained oblivious. She hated that Micah had gone through such a heartbreak and that his heart had been forever damaged. He deserved better. *Like you?* a voice she ignored whispered.

"Thank you for sharing all this with me," she told him softly.

"You're welcome. I'm normally not so open, but I trust you."

"You can," she reassured him. She'd *never* betray him. Her loyal nature forbade it. Besides, she liked him a great deal more than she should. "We're sort of friends."

"I know and I'm glad of it." His self-assurance could be her undoing. He was a man who knew what he wanted and what he was about. "I have a gut instinct about people who work for me, and I just knew when I read your résumé that we would be a good fit, and I was right. You've been a perfect addition to the office. Thanks for letting me confide in you."

His words made her stomach flutter. But then she gave herself a mental shake. They were business colleagues, nothing more. "You're welcome. I appreciate all you do for me."

He glanced at his watch, which was one of those expensive, classic brands that graced the wrists of celebrities and professional athletes. He groaned. "Where did the time go? It's almost four. We should get back to the office so you can go home. I'm sure everyone's cleared out already for the holiday."

Micah had given his staff Good Friday through Easter Monday off, providing a four-day weekend. Anything essential or needing immediate attention could be done remotely. Jacinta stood and retrieved her water glass.

She edged around the coffee table and, as she did, the point of her closed-toe shoe caught on the wicker and she stumbled as her ankle twisted. Micah was there in an instant to steady her as the glass slipped from her fingers and landed safely on the couch. "I got you," he said, wrapping an arm around her. "Steady there."

"Thanks." His arm was a comforting weight causing her body to short circuit. She was petite next to him, and he was hard and lean and male. His ex was a complete fool, Jacinta decided. So was she for not having moved away yet. She tried to step out of his magnetic proximity and out from between the table and the love seat, but as her ankle bent again, she fell even further into Micah's embrace and her face nuzzled into his shirt.

If she were a romance movie heroine, this would be the moment of the almost kiss. The charged thought made Jacinta gaze upward and, to her shock, found they were on the same wavelength. He gathered her closer to him.

"We'll wiggle out," he suggested. "Okay with you?"

"Sure," she whispered. They shuffled sideways, pressed together, out from between the furnishings. However, once in the open, he made no move to release her. Instead, his eyes darkened and strands of Micah's hair swooped forward when his forehead bent toward hers. The light rain provided a soothing backdrop, and without thinking, Jacinta licked her lips. The arm with the watch lifted and he pushed some of her hair behind her ear. His finger lightly traced her jawline and he stooped further. Then, as if his actions had shocked him, he drew back and put distance between them. "You good?"

"I am. I've got it from here," she said, the obvious chemistry dissipating. "I appreciate your help. I'm normally in tennis shoes when I'm in the chocolate factory. But they didn't match my outfit so I wore these closed-toe beauties instead. I should have known better and dressed appropriately." But she'd wanted to appear professional for both him and her grandmother.

"As long as your ankle is okay, wear what you want. Do you need some ice?" He retrieved the wayward glass.

"No, I'm good." Jacinta made an exaggerated stomp with her foot. "Works. Nothing to see here." Taking the initiative, she led the way into the kitchen, where she grabbed her purse. "Thank you for letting me see your house. By the time I get home, Abuela will have shut down and started dinner. Minus some coursework I need to complete, I get to relax this weekend."

Micah set the glass in the sink. "I hope you have a nice Easter."

"Me, too. It'll be what it is." When they reached the front door, the rain magically ended, as if the sky didn't dare spit on a member of the Fortune family. "Hopefully, I can wade through the 'How are you doing on getting married' questions."

Micah pulled the front door shut. "If you sense an opening, I'm serious about investing. The worst that can happen is she says no."

"True." In the car, Jacinta secured her seat belt. When Micah started the engine, she brightened. "Oh, I like this song."

"He and his wife were at the guest ranch a few months ago," Micah said, and conversation turned to matters other than the fact that she'd been in his arms, his head had been coming down toward hers and, if they hadn't worked together, he might have kissed her.

And she would definitely have kissed him back.

As they drove into town, as if by unspoken agreement, neither of them brought up the almost kiss. Pretending nothing was amiss was the way to go, Jacinta decided. If Micah could ignore the fact each of them had desired the other, so could she. They worked together. No need to complicate things...they each had enough on their plates already. She had bigger issues—like finding a husband or finding a new career—than worrying about an almost kiss.

But none of that could hide the truth. She'd been willing to complicate her working relationship and raise the stakes. She'd wanted his kiss.

Even more amazing, he'd wanted it, too.

Chapter Five

By the time the caterers cleared the last of the Fortunes'
Sunday dinner, Micah had reached his family saturation
point. He'd attended the annual Easter egg hunt earlier in
the day. Because his cousins had their future spouses with
them, the number at the day's events had grown. Naomi
was with Shane, and all the women had oohed and aahed
and studied her finger as if they'd never seen a diamond before. Then Poppy, who was engaged to Leo Leonetti, CEO
of the famous Texas winery, had discussed their upcoming
nuptials, and of course Micah's mom had gone gaga over
Baby Joey, who was now a little over two months old. She'd
then looked Micah directly in the eye and asked when he'd
be giving her grandchildren.

Uncomfortable hadn't even begun to describe that sin-
gular moment, and he'd shoved a large bite of coconut cake
into his mouth to avoid answering. The icing was so sweet,
he'd almost gagged, but the trick had worked. He'd hoped
his mother would pose the question next of his siblings,
which she had, of course. Instead of eating cake, his sister, Vivienne, sipped the port wine Leo had brought from
his vineyards. Younger brother Drake had given a half-
hearted, "Mom, stop pressuring me or it'll never happen."

Micah had never been so grateful when everyone retired
to the family room and the women grouped together, with

the exception of his sister, Vivienne, who joined the men so they could discuss ranch business. "Have we made any progress with the thefts?" Micah's dad asked. Even though their dad had stepped away from the company, he remained deeply committed to the ranch, which had been in the Fortune family since the 1800s. When it became time for the next generation, Micah's dad's cousin Garth had taken over the guest ranch operations while Hayden had built the cattle operation and stables.

"We're working on it," Vivienne assured him. She pushed some of her blond hair off her face. Forewoman of Fortune's Gold cattle operation, Micah's sister often boasted she rode horses better than he did, which was a distinct possibility, not that they'd ever put the theory to the test. As CEO, Micah appreciated how much his hardworking sister loved the ranch. Five years ago, she'd earned their father's trust and become foreman. He and his family couldn't ask for anyone better to run operations.

"Micah's planning on going uncover as a ranch hand. I'm planting the seeds for the fact we need another hand now," Vivienne added.

Their father nodded. "It'll be good to have someone's boots on the ground, on the inside."

Micah sipped his finger of bourbon. "I agree. I want an impenetrable disguise and the last piece is scheduled to arrive soon. If the crew know I'm a Fortune, they're not going to talk to me."

"True," Hayden agreed. He turned to Shane. "Still no word on your horse?"

Shane shook his head. "No. Haven't seen it come up for auction. I've got people watching."

"As do I," Vivienne said. "But in good news, the calving is finished, and we've got a quality herd. Micah ensured that the cattle we shipped to Argentina arrived safely. Feed-back is our clients are pleased. If we don't count the sab-otage and thefts, things are running well. And, as I said, hopefully we'll get that stopped soon."

Hayden rubbed his fingers over the gray five-o'clock shadow gracing his chin. "What about the association din-ner?" he asked Micah. "While that's a ways off, we also have that dinner meeting with Alan Bess and his wife. Are you going to attend by yourself again?"

Micah set his bourbon glass down. "I hadn't planned on bringing a date."

His dad refrained from rolling his eyes, but Micah sensed the gesture anyway. "I don't want to agree with your mother, but even numbers work best. The least you could do is bring someone so that the women can sit at the end of the table and we don't have an empty seat."

"I'm sure I can find someone," Micah said. "I could bring Vivienne."

This time his father did glance heavenward first. "No, we don't want this to appear as if the Fortunes are trying to dominate. You need a date." For a moment, his dad appeared to rethink what he was about to say, but then he plowed ahead. "If you were married, this wouldn't be an issue…"

"Not you, too," Micah groaned. "Besides wanting a grandchild, I heard enough tonight from Mom."

As if sensing a deluge coming, the rest of the group melted away.

"Look, son," his dad said when they were alone. "I know I'm going to sound old-fashioned, but you're thirty-four."

"And?" Micah prompted. "I'm not over the hill or any-thing."

"No, but that's not the point," his dad argued. "The fact is that we work in a very traditional male-dominated industry, with your sister being a rare exception. You know I believe that women are equal to men, and your sister has managed the ranch better than any of the previous foremen. But the fact remains that many men of your stature are married. A single man, especially a Fortune, can be intimidating."

In the mirror across the way, Micah could see his expression mimicked that time he'd bitten into a stale sour candy. "Gee, thanks. Everyone who knows me in a business capacity knows that I'm decisive but fair. I have no toleration for stupidity or inefficiency, or illegality, but I make it a point not to intimidate people. That's the last impression I want to give."

"You're missing my point. You, son, are rich. You're handsome. Almost too good-looking. You are successful, extremely so. Women find that very attractive, even married women."

Micah bristled. "You know I don't cheat and I certainly don't sleep with married women."

His dad shook his head. "Of course not. But being a bachelor makes you a target. Men feel threatened, worried that their wives may want you. Even if their wives don't want you sexually, the idea that they might, all by itself, can create doubt in some of our clients' minds about their own self-worth. It's about optics."

"This has to be the biggest load of…" Biting his tongue before he could say BS, Micah failed to find the right polite words to use. Was he about to say "malarkey"? Then he'd be as old-fashioned as his father. "People are marrying later these days. What if I were a widower? Like Rafe?"

"Rafe is now happily engaged to Heidi. The point is that you are single. *Very single.* And not only are you attractive, you are a Fortune. The sooner you marry, the better."

"That's absurd," Micah protested. The idea was ludicrous.

His dad remained unapologetic. "It's just the way things are. It's unfair, and I don't agree with it, but it's the way it is. The way of the world is often wrong, but to survive, we have to conform. I know you've always been above reproach, but at times I've heard whispers. Innuendos. One angry client who gets the wrong idea is all it takes, even if it's not true. Look at what happened to Garth."

"And having a wife fixes that?" Micah twisted his lips and jerked a hand through his hair. "Ridiculous."

"Optics," his father repeated. "You are a man in a traditional CEO role. If you had a wife, that would make you a part of a respectable couple. Men won't feel so threatened."

"Ridiculous," Micah repeated. It was that or cuss up a storm. "Women want me because I'm a Fortune. I don't want them back. There's no problem. No issue."

"Not in your mind. But having a wife would help fend those women off. Make life easier on all of us."

Micah shook his head. The very idea of marriage was the antithesis of what he wanted right now. Especially after being betrayed as he had.

"No one is saying you must marry immediately, least of all me," his dad continued. "But you do need to lose the 'I'll never marry' stance and realize that life is passing you by, and that the longer you wait, the more harm it might do to your reputation and career. Besides, you're beginning to get to that permanent bachelor stage where people start to wonder if there's something wrong with you. Like, if no woman wants you, maybe you're deficient somehow."

"I am *not* deficient." Micah folded his arms across his chest and hoped that eventually his dad would lose steam and end this nonsense.

"I know there's nothing wrong with you, but being a CEO means people's perceptions matter."

"Who the hell cares what—"

"Just think it over, son. I'm not saying you need to race to the altar." His dad grinned. "That's your mother. She's been dying to plan a wedding for one of her own kids, especially after listening to Shelley titter on and on."

"Fine. I'll take what you said under advisement," Micah gritted out. Despite his irritation, his father did have a point in one regard. Micah had had married women hit on him and single ones as well. While having a wife wouldn't be necessarily a guaranteed deterrent, he could see the benefits of how a woman could diffuse another woman's attempts. However, that was as far as Micah's considerations of his dad's outrageous idea went. He wasn't dating, not that he was a monk by any means. But after the betrayal, he'd decided career came first. He was too busy with being the CEO, trying to stop the sabotage and worrying about how to help Jacinta, than to find a wife—which he didn't want anyway, thank you very much.

He now understood how Jacinta must have felt with Abuela giving her the ultimatum and threatening to take away her dream. Hayden hadn't given him a specific directive, but Micah had felt the pressure anyway. If nothing else, he had to come up with a date to the business dinner. A picture of Jacinta and her beauty flickered through his mind. Brushing aside the fact he'd almost kissed her earlier today, which had been an aberration on both of their parts that *wouldn't* happen again, she'd be a safe, perfect companion to take to the dinner with Alan Bess. Bess was a broker representing some wealthy ranchers in Montana who had taken an interest in buying some Fortune cattle. "I'll bring a date to the dinner," he told his father, tossing him at least one bone. "You don't need to worry about the table being an odd number, god forbid."

"Excellent," his dad said. "When my administrative assistant gets the time and location set, I'll have her contact yours." With that, his father moved off to speak with his wife.

Micah's sister, Vivienne, arched an eyebrow as she moseyed back over. "Did I just hear you say you're bringing a date to the dinner with Alan Bess?"

Micah's first response was to say, "Don't start with me," with his second, "Is that so hard to believe?" Instead, he merely said, "Yes. Why, yes, I am."

Then a thought caught hold in the back recesses of his brain and, as it took root, a plan began to form. As the idea moved to the forefront, Micah realized he might have a solution to both his and Jacinta's problem.

All he needed her to do was say yes.

Jacinta found Easter dinner as fraught as the previous weekend's meal, the one where Abuela had made her declaration that Jacinta must marry or else. Over a meal of shrimp empanadas de vigilia, Jacinta listened as Sofia boldly lied about how she was planning on keeping everything the same. Jacinta remained quiet until the prattle got on her last nerves. That's when she sweetly looked at her cousin and said, "You told me at the restaurant you were going to sell the entire business. Has that changed?"

But instead of Jacinta trapping Sofia into revealing her plan to build condos, Abuela rose to her granddaughter's defense. "That's her prerogative. I don't want to expand, and your cousin has young children she's responsible for. You don't know what's going on in her world, her life."

"You don't mean that," Jacinta protested, hurt by Abuela's reaction. Her grandmother could not be serious. Even Sofia appeared shocked by the depth of Rosa's stubbornness.

"I do. If Sofia wants to sell to make a better life for her family, so be it," Abuela reiterated.

Remembering Micah's offer, Jacinta used the weapon he'd handed her. "Fine. Sell it to me. I'll offer you one hundred thousand for it. Two hundred if it appraises for that."

For a moment, no one had said anything, until Sofia sputtered, "Where would you even get that type of a loan? Even with a business plan, no bank will lend to you."

"I'm respectfully speaking to Abuela." Jacinta stared at her grandmother, who slowly shook her head.

"I don't like the two of you fighting. You're family. Perhaps it's better to let the company go to an outsider, if nothing else to stop this division between us. So, I'm sorry, but my answer is no. In fact, let me show you these." Abuela stood and grabbed a set of papers bound by brads and a blue cover. "I've already had the transfer plans drawn up. All I need to tell the lawyer is whose name to put on the documents. Yours if you marry. Sofia's otherwise."

Well, Jacinta thought morosely, that put her in her place.

She relayed the entire story on Monday when she met her friends for lunch. "And that was that."

"Has she gone senile?" Kim asked.

"No. I wish the explanation for her behavior could be that simple, but she's fine. Not that I want her senile." Despite her grandmother's behavior, Jacinta loved her abuela too much to wish for that.

"We know what you mean," Carolyn soothed. She topped off Jacinta's glass of wine.

"She's just so headstrong and won't back down. I even brought up how Micah Fortune is single and no one's giving him grief, and you know what she said?"

"No, what?" Kim, Carolyn and Katie asked in unison.

"She said that's okay for men and not women!" Jacinta

leaned back with a thump. At her suggestion, they'd chosen to meet at Francesca's because Jacinta had wanted to try more of the delicious food and support one of Micah's investments.

"Well, that sounds senile to me," Kim said. "Rosa's never had that *patriarchy is better* stance before. She's one of the most pro-women, you-go-girl cheerleaders I know. Remember how she told me that I shouldn't let Andrew hold me back? She was the one that told me he was gaslighting me, and she was right! How can she have flipped the script on you like this?"

Jacinta had resorted to twisting the linen napkin again. "I don't know, but something made her dig in. How am I supposed to get married in such a short period of time?"

"You need a convenient groom," Carolyn suggested.

"A what?" Jacinta swiveled in her friend's direction.

Carolyn shrugged. "A marriage of convenience. Find a guy you trust, draw up some legal paperwork, pretend to be in love and marry him. Abuela never said anything about you getting divorced, did she?"

"No, but the idea is crazy." Jacinta couldn't believe she was considering it. "Real life is not a movie. And I'm not copulating with some guy I'm married to so I can get the business."

"Which is why a no-sex clause goes in the legal paperwork," Carolyn said practically. "No one's saying you have to sleep with him. Just marry him and write a divorce date into the deal. You get the company. He gets…well, we can work on that."

"If my brother wasn't overseas, he'd do it," Katie said. "He's due some leave from the marines. He could swoop in and save the day. That's what he's trained for."

"No. I might be desperate, but your brother is twenty-one. I'm not making him a divorcee by age twenty-two."

"You'd be sisters," Carolyn pointed out.

"Even more reason. Imagine how awkward that would be at family gatherings. 'Oh hi, Oskar's new girlfriend. This is my best friend, his ex-wife.' No. Just no." Jacinta's nose wrinkled. "Besides, I'd have to kiss him and that would make things weird." She shivered as if someone had walked over her grave and wrung her hands. "This isn't helping. I'm not marrying Katie's brother. I can't imagine kissing him. Sorry, Katie."

"No worries. I wouldn't want to kiss him either. You need to find someone you *want* to kiss."

That answer was easy. Micah. She'd been in his arms. Like slow-motion replay, Jacinta remembered the way his lips had lowered toward hers. Her own had parted before they'd both come to their senses and stepped away. Thankfully, when they'd returned to the office, they'd gone their separate ways. Certainly by tomorrow the aberrations of the last week would have worn off. Maybe not for her situation with Abuela, but definitely for her and Micah.

She changed the subject. "Did I tell you both that Micah offered me money to buy out Abuela? It would be a business deal. He's a silent investor in this place."

"But would she even sell?" Kim asked. "Will she calm down after last night and think it through?"

Jacinta's puckered lips provided her answer.

"Of course not, because her grandmother is foolish and shortsighted to demand this of a modern woman." Katie patted Jacinta on the arm. "We're sorry, sweetie. You don't deserve this."

"No, but I have one last card, and I'll level it when the time is right. I doubt it will change her mind, but I have to try."

"As long as you've considered all possibilities…" Kim said.

She'd done nothing but. "I have. I can go to work for the

Fortunes. Not for Micah, but somewhere else. He told me that he would find me a position somewhere in the Fortune companies that's worthy of my talents and my degree."

"That's fabulous! You landed a great mentor." Carolyn reached for the bill folio the server had set down. Jacinta glanced at her own and slid her credit card inside.

"I'm fortunate, no pun intended." Her attempt at lightening the moment didn't quite succeed.

"You are. So, what is your next step? What's the card you're going to play?" Katie asked.

"Moving out."

"Really? I'd say it's about time to do that anyway," Kim said.

"I didn't want her to be alone, and I was finishing grad school," Jacinta said defensively. "But yeah, if I'm losing the chocolate company, I'm not staying in her house. She doesn't get to run my life any longer."

"That's wise," Carolyn agreed. "You working for the Fortunes with Micah's recommendation is like writing your own ticket. Isn't it?"

"I'll talk to him tomorrow." Jacinta glanced at her friends. "I'm twenty-six and ready for my life to begin. No reason for me to stay at Abuela's if I won't be working in the backyard."

Carolyn nodded. "Great idea. She's used to having you there. She doesn't want you to leave."

"She wants you married," Kim reminded her. "Which means you'd leave anyway."

"But not in the way she wants. Enough's enough."

"Yeah, her actions have consequences," Katie said.

Jacinta nodded. "Exactly. I love her, but this is *my* life. She refuses to back down? Well, she's not seen anything yet. *Una mujer exitosa es aquella que puede sentar una base firme con los ladrillos que otros le han arrojado.*"

"You know I don't speak a word of Spanish," Katie complained.

"She said a successful woman is one who can lay a firm foundation with the bricks others have thrown at her," Kim translated.

"Exactly," Jacinta said, thinking of the pavers that lined the driveway to the Fortune's Gold Guest Ranch and Spa. Micah believed she could do it. "I will build something better."

But some of her earlier bravado faded once she was in the car, but she shook it off as she drove home. She went into her room, closed the door and began to finish her final term paper. She'd learned long ago that a person didn't get everything they wanted. If they did, her parents would be alive.

While it wouldn't be easy, she'd swallow this bitter pill and somehow keep it from poisoning her from the inside out. She'd apply the lesson from one of her MBA courses, the one where the professor had students study the origin of famous quotes about success and failure.

While some had chosen people such as Henry Ford, Thomas Edison or even Bill Gates, Jacinta had picked a quote by Alexander Graham Bell. Most knew the phrase when one door closes another one opens, or something about opening a window instead. But Bell's full quote had been *When one door closes another door opens; but we so often look so long and so regretfully upon the closed door, that we do not see the ones which open for us.*

The door to Jacinta's owning Abuela Rosa Chocolates was closed. But Micah was opening another one for her. Time to line up a career-building job, finish her degree and move out and onward.

Whether Abuela liked it or not.

Chapter Six

To Jacinta's disappointment, when she arrived to work on Tuesday, she discovered that Micah had sent an email relaying that he had an emergency meeting out at the ranch and that he wouldn't be in until noon. He'd asked her to order his and her favorite sandwiches from the Emerald Ridge Café and to be prepared for a working lunch.

Jacinta placed the delivery order online and tapped her fingers idly against the keyboard. She could wait a few more hours to speak with him. She normally wasn't this impatient. But now that she'd made her decision, she was ready to put a plan in place. To ensure they had enough time to discuss her job situation, she added an extra fifteen minutes onto the hour for lunch Micah had allotted in calendar. That would still give him thirty minutes before his scheduled meeting with the sales team.

The food arrived at eleven forty-five and Micah strolled in ten minutes later. Depending on the type of meeting and number of people, Jacinta would sometimes book a conference room. Because it was the two of them and she planned to take him up on his offer to find her a job, she'd arranged the food on the four-foot square table in Micah's office. She'd placed herself to his right. Since the Emerald Ridge Café served boxed luncheons, the only things she'd set out were a bottle of water for her and a can of iced tea for Micah.

Micah set his briefcase on his desk and approached. The little zing of anticipation was surely because of what she had to tell him, not because he looked so handsome in his cowboy boots, fitted jeans and a tight T-shirt topped with a flannel long-sleeve. "Everything go well at the ranch?" she asked.

"Yeah." He settled onto the leather rolling chair. "Vivienne wanted my help moving a herd of cattle to another pasture. She was right. We found some places where the barbed-wire fencing had been snipped. It was only the top strand, and barbed wire can snap if it's too tight or takes some force, but this looked cut. Luckily none of our cattle tried to walk through it, which they might do since their head could go over it. But the herd was fine and we've moved them to a safe location."

"You think it's more sabotage?" Tiredness ringed his eyes, as if he'd been awake most of the night.

"Looks like. I got the call around three a.m. We think the person might have been scared off. Because the wire has pressure and tension, any cutting has to be done carefully. We've upped security, so maybe that's all the perpetrator could do before something spooked him. Or maybe he's just trying to cause us grief."

"Either way, it's time and profit and stress," Jacinta observed.

"Absolutely." Micah opened his lunch box. His favorite order was the roast beef sandwich on Texas toast that came with lettuce, tomato and Swiss cheese. Instead of a bag of chips, he had pasta salad. Jacinta had a turkey club croissant with a side salad. Each meal came with a dill pickle spear and a homemade chocolate-chip cookie. Micah dove into his sandwich, using the red-and-white-paper wrapper as a plate. He motioned for her to unwrap her food, too. Complying, Jacinta set out her spread, knowing her boss would want to eat and make polite chitchat before getting down to actual new business. His reasoning? Because if things ever got too fraught or negotiations became impossible, then at least he had a full stomach if he had to walk out.

While they ate, they discussed the Easter weekend. Micah told her about how much Baby Joey had grown. Jacinta shared how she'd spent her days off by finishing her final term paper and having lunch with her best friends. "What do they do again?" he asked.

"Carolyn is a teacher in Emerald Ridge. Kim owns a public relations firm. Katie manages the art gallery."

"Oh, I've been there. I once bought my mom some fancy piece of raku pottery she fell in love with for Mother's Day. Do you know how hard it is to buy something for a person who has everything?" He paused. "Sorry. That may have come out insensitive."

"No, it's fine. I was little when my mom passed. It doesn't hurt when people talk about their moms, but I appreciate you thinking of my feelings." His doing so showed yet another way he truly was perfect. "And you've met Abuela. Can you imagine how hard it is to purchase things for her? She's the pickiest person I know. Because she wants things to be just right, she was even throwing out the broken chocolate, until I told her that was wasteful and that we could sell it as imperfect-looking but perfect-tasting and that people would purchase it. And they do."

Micah grinned. "Perfect chocolate is overrated. I put my chocolate bars in the refrigerator. Then I break them into jagged pieces before I remove them from the wrapper. It's a quirk. I tell myself I'm only going to have one broken section, but then I'll eat half, put the wrapper back, and then I'll go back ten minutes later and finish."

She held up her thumb and forefinger like pinchers. "You know those peanut butter cup candies, the minisized ones? I bite the top off, eat that part first and then I stick the bottom half into my mouth."

His laughter was like her favorite slippers, all warm and fuzzy. "We each have our candy idiosyncrasies. That means I'm not alone in being abnormal. Thanks for being weird with me."

"We are *not* weird," she admonished playfully. "We're just different in our approaches. Nothing wrong with that." She waited as Micah began removing the cookie from the wrapper. The protective sleeve rustled. "Micah, there's something I…"

"Jacinta, I wanted to talk to you about…"

As they were both talking at the same time, they stopped and glanced at each other. Micah gave her a little wave. "After you."

Her cheeks heated. "No, go ahead. You're the boss."

"But it's ladies first." The wink he gave her made her nerves zing.

"Okay. Here goes." She slid her box toward the center of the table. "I did some thinking this weekend, and I'd like to take you up on your offer to find me a job."

His eyes lit up with interest but he remained silent, waiting for her to go on.

"You've offered to find me an incredible opportunity and I'd be a fool not to take you up on it. I've realized that I've been spending so much time looking at what I don't have that I'm being shortsighted in regards to what's in front of me." She took a breath before continuing. "If Abuela wants to give Sofia the company and Sofia sells it, I have to be okay with that. I must be willing to let it go. Which means, as soon as I get my degree, it's time for me to leave my childhood home and move on with my life. I don't need to remain beholden, and I certainly don't need to get married."

Micah nodded thoughtfully. "True. But what if getting married would allow you to have everything you wanted?"

"That would be nice, but as we've already established, I'm not dating anyone." She bit into her cookie. Delicious dessert therapy.

Micah swallowed, the movement bringing her gaze to his throat. She yanked her eyes upward as he gave her a sheepish smile. "Turns out I might need help in the marriage mart area myself. I figured that perhaps we could help each other out."

Jacinta's heart leapt. *Wait, what?* Micah was interested in her? When? How? Her brain waited for the punchline, the rest of the story. It came immediately. "My father told me I needed to have a date for the Alan Bess dinner, which is not this Friday but the one after that. So I thought of you."

The quivering excitement she felt didn't dissipate, but it did lessen. From the gleam in his eye, Jacinta could tell he was approaching his dating problem from an analytical perspective, not from an "I've fallen for my intern" realization.

"While I'm happy to attend a business dinner with you, how would me being there work? Your father knows me as your intern. If I'm there to even the table numbers, that's one thing. But if it's to pretend to be your girlfriend, that's quite another. It's unethical." Even if showing up somewhere as Micah's date created fairy-tale vibes. She'd read *Cinderella*. At times being discovered by a rich Prince Charming held great appeal.

"I considered those things, which led me to another even more radical proposition. In business, we like to say it's best to kill two birds with one stone. Saves resources and time. In my case, I have the resources and the time. You don't have the resources or the time, at least not where your grandmother is concerned. But what if you married? What if you married *me*?"

Jacinta swore her mouth dropped open. Silence fell. She somehow managed to find her voice. "I don't understand…" While marrying Micah would be a princess fantasy come true, Jacinta stared at her boss like he'd blurted out that he wanted to fly them both to Mars. "We work together. You have a reputation to maintain."

A nonchalant shrug accompanied his, "Yes, and that wouldn't change. I'm suggesting a purely platonic, short-term marriage of convenience. We'll marry by your deadline, depriving your cousin of parsing out the company. And as your husband, no one will think twice about me investing in your company, which I would be, allowing you to expand according to the business plan you created." He cleared his throat and hesitated a moment, as if measuring his next words carefully. "If you want bank funding, my last name carries a lot of weight in this town, even if you choose to keep your own last name, as I know many women do."

Stunned by his frank proposal, Jacinta glanced anywhere in the office except at Micah. Her gaze flickered over his framed diplomas, which hung next to a series of plaques—mostly awards from local and state business organizations. He had an original Georgia O'Keeffe on one wall and a landscape of blue bonnets painted by Porfirio Salinas. He'd once told her that while Salinas had been born in Texas, the Wisconsin-born O'Keeffe had established her Texas roots in Canyon, where she'd been a professor at West Texas A&M.

"Jacinta?" Micah prompted. "I know I've shocked you,

but I don't mean anything untoward. We would live in name only. You've seen my house. You could have your own wing."

It struck her then how totally serious he was. Her friends had suggested a marriage of convenience to Katie's brother, and here Micah was proposing the same thing. But to *him* instead. The man she wanted to kiss. And far more. "For one thing, I'd be lying to my grandmother and that's all sorts of wrong."

Micah fingered his napkin. "Not if we were married. Legal paperwork and all. That's not lying. She doesn't need to know what we do behind closed doors."

"She wants me married for love." Could he love her? She dismissed the thought as ridiculous. He'd said his heart was closed.

"If your grandmother wanted you to marry for love, she would have given you more than six weeks, especially when she knows you're not dating anyone."

He had her there.

"She also would have not threatened to take away your hopes and dreams as incentive," Micah continued. "That borders on all sorts of wrong. I'm not saying she doesn't love you, but she shouldn't be controlling you in this way for her own selfish reasons. Your life is your own, Jacinta, and if we marry, I'll ensure it stays that way."

She'd go from one roommate—her grandmother—to another. But if marrying Micah got her out of the house and achieved her goal of owning the chocolate company... Wouldn't that be a win-win? Nothing, however, ever came without strings. "What's in it for you?" she asked. "There has to be something. Because, from my angle, you're not getting sex and there's no guarantee my company will even meet its financial goals. Business plans are based on hypotheticals, and you could lose a lot of money backing me. Why are you doing this? It's an outrageous proposition."

"Yeah, I know. But, at Easter, my dad pointed out a hard truth. He reminded me that in this old-fashioned, patriarchal-driven world, it's sometimes better if a man has a wife. Being married will make the men I'm around feel more comfortable. For some reason my dad believes I'm a love magnet, or at least the men in my orbit are afraid that their wives are all lusting after me."

He did sort of look like a younger David Beckham, she reminded herself. And as Kim, Katie and Carolyn had mentioned, Micah was smoking hot. While Jacinta couldn't argue with his father's logic, she could in principle. "While that's a reasonable assumption, it's simply all sorts of wrong. First, we both know you're not the kind to cheat or abuse anyone's trust."

"I'm not, and I appreciate your faith in me, which is one reason why, when he mentioned dating or marrying, you came to mind. I never planned on marrying. Being once burned makes me twice shy."

"I get where you're coming from, but it sounds ridiculous. As ridiculous as the situation I'm in." Although, her friends had suggested a marriage of convenience. But used to being independent, she hadn't given the idea much credence. Well, not a lot anyway. "There's not another option?"

He sighed. "Perhaps, but not enough time for either of us to find it. With my cousins now all engaged, I've got at least three weddings in my future. I'll stick out like a sore thumb without a date. Not to mention the dinner with Alan Bess and his wife and my parents. And there's the association dinner. So when you ask me what I'm getting out of it? I'm getting people to leave me the hell alone and let me live my life the way I want. I believe you can empathize and understand that."

"I can." It was strange to think that the all-powerful Micah Fortune had real-world problems, too, at least those beyond the stuff happening at the ranch. "This is incredible but I'm going to have to think about it."

"Understood. How about we talk more tonight over dinner?" Micah suggested.

"Can't. I've got class. Thankfully, I'm done with those after this week, minus finishing the internship, which is technically over at the end of next week."

"How about you plan to stay on, at least until I can get you transferred? But if you get the chocolate company…" His voice trailed off. "I have a meeting tomorrow night, so how about dinner on Thursday? The business shindig is the following Friday. I'll arrange for you to take my credit card and get a dress."

"I can't accept a—"

He cut her off. "You can. Even if you say no to marrying me, you'll be doing me a favor by attending as my date. Consider a dress a graduation gift and putting some of my money back into the local economy."

Jacinta knew she wasn't going to convince him otherwise. He could be as stubborn as Abuela at times. "Okay. Dinner Thursday and we'll work out the details, if there *are* details to be worked out. Either way, I'll go to the Alan Bess dinner with you to keep things even. I can do you that favor."

"Perfect." He glanced at watch. "I'm due to meet with the salesforce."

"Yes. I'll clean up in here…"

"Great. Thank you." He pointed a finger her way. "Think about what I said. Mum's the word until we decide. If we do this, everyone must believe it's real. That's something you should consider seriously when you make your decision. And, Jacinta, there's one more thing…"

"Yeah? What is it?" she asked softly.

"I will be faithful to you. I'd ask that you do the same. We'd both be giving up our physical needs."

"I understand." Seeing she was serious, Micah nodded once before walking out. Jacinta cleaned the remains of lunch. She couldn't believe what Micah had proposed. No wonder he was so successful. He seemed to have an answer for everything. But a marriage of convenience? Yesterday the idea was ludicrous. Crazy. Absurd. There were a million words she could think of to describe why the idea was, at its core, dumb. Her friends had been joking.

However, coming from Micah, the idea had merit and would solve both of their problems. Was it considered lying to Abuela if she was legally married? That was a conundrum. She had two days to think about Micah's proposal. She'd draw up a pro-con list and weigh each side. And she'd also come up with list of questions. A draft of her terms. As for the no-sex part? She was no anticipatory virgin who needed a wedding night. Jacinta didn't do casual sex, and she hadn't had a serious boyfriend in ages. Extending her celibacy streak shouldn't be an issue.

Even if she did want his kiss.

Because of issues at the ranch involving deliveries from a new feed supplier, Micah and Jacinta's Thursday-night dinner date became lunch in the office the following Wednesday afternoon, exactly a week and a day from their last meal together. He'd decided that was for the best. He'd sent her final internship review to her professor, giving her the highest marks. Since they weren't yet engaged, there could be no accusation of impropriety on his part as her mentor. He worried about things like that.

He'd found her a new position in the company, and he'd offer that to her today. If she agreed, she'd start that job next week. Last night, he'd walked into the two spare bedrooms on the other side of his house and decided that Jacinta could use one for her office and the other for her bedroom. She could redecorate them to fit her aesthetic. He'd also spoken to his lawyer, a college buddy whom he trusted completely and worked for him alone. Micah wanted no scandalous hint that his and Jacinta's marriage would not be real. To the outside world and both of their families, their marriage needed to appear as loving and proper as his parents' marriage was.

"Hey," Jacinta said. He studied her as she entered his office carrying a delivery bag. She was gorgeous and his fingers longed to run themselves through the long straight strands that fell to her midback. His libido felt a small pang that their marriage wouldn't include sex.

"Let me take that," he offered, reaching out a hand.

She brushed him aside with an, "I've got it. Sit down."

"Okay." He'd make things awkward between them if he didn't, so he pulled out a chair and lowered himself onto it. She reached into the bag, making her short-sleeved sweater inch up. He caught a hint of sun-kissed skin before she lowered her arms and handed him a box. His libido awakened, Micah busied himself with unpacking his lunch. Once again, he'd gotten his favorite from the Emerald Ridge Café. Perhaps he should shake things up once in a while. He waited until she sat down. "I spoke with my lawyer."

He noted she didn't appear surprised or offended. "I assumed you'd want a prenup," she said.

Micah hastened to explain. "To avoid bad feelings, it

would be better if we outlined the full terms of our marriage and its eventual dissolution, make things cleaner if they are spelled out so we both know what to expect. The sample document is in that envelope, along with a cover sheet of highlights."

Jacinta slid the manila envelope toward her and withdrew one sheet. Her eyebrows knit together and a little wrinkle formed. She set the paper down. "This is far too generous."

"Frankly, I don't believe it's enough. When we walk away in a year, you'll be the ex-wife of a Fortune. That can have its own stigma, both good and bad. If you're not taken care of, that reflects poorly on me and my family. At that same time, you'll also be the one who couldn't keep a Fortune happy. You deserve to be compensated for any looks of pity you might receive and any gossip you might endure, no matter how friendly and civil our uncoupling."

As was habit when she was thinking, she nibbled her lower lip. He wanted to reach out and draw her hand way. "I hadn't thought of those things. There's a lot to unwrap here…"

"How so?" He wanted her to say yes, but he also wanted her to see the complete picture of what her future might look like should she marry him. "What questions do you have?"

"I'm wondering what people will think of me? What my grandmother will think? No one in my family has ever been divorced, and I'd be the first."

"Are you thinking there's a shame in that?" Micah hadn't considered that angle. While he'd ruminated on their living together, he'd assumed they'd be more like college roommates who went separate ways when the term ended.

"In a way, yes, it's slightly shameful. I'm not the kind who thinks things could be better by having more money.

And I don't like taking a payout even if you have a bottomless well of cash."

That was one reason he adored her. He shot her a cheeky grin. "I'm not sure I have that much."

Refusing to let him tease his way out of this, Jacinta gave a quick shake of her head. "Close enough. But the amount you offered is outrageous to a woman of my upbringing. You're giving me a lump sum and the business free and clear. It's excessive."

Micah worked to convince her of his good intentions. "I consider the amount more than fair. You're doing me a favor…and I'm investing in you, Jacinta. I believe in you and want you to succeed. I can't promise you love, but I can give you what you need. What you want. Your dream."

"I still don't know what *you* want."

What if what he wanted was her? The thought hit him like whiplash—arriving out of nowhere and seen at the last second. He cleared his throat as she returned the typed sheet to the envelope.

She pointed to a line. "I can't believe your lawyer added that part about us having kids when the physical isn't part of this. Or that he added the infidelity parts."

Micah's libido jumped at the idea of being intimate with Jacinta. He was attracted to her, plain and simple, but he was also a gentleman. As for the infidelity? After what had happened to him, he could never imagine doing that to anyone else.

"Those are standard clauses. That's his job, to think of all possibilities. I said we were marrying fast and didn't dissuade his belief that we'd fallen in love almost overnight. That we're doing this for our own personal reasons is our business and ours alone."

"On that I agree." She moved a fork from one side of

the empty wrapper to the other, as if giving her nervous energy an outlet.

He tilted his head and studied her. "You agree on what? With it being our business or you're agreeing to marry me?"

"Both," Jacinta said. She lifted her sandwich and then put it back down again. "I'm glad you met with the lawyer. I'm glad things are spelled out. In order for me to do this, we must handle this like a business deal. We sign papers. We see the judge. Then we have three-, six- and nine-month checkups and performance reviews. If either of us think that something isn't working at those meetings, we deal with our issues then. At the eleven-month mark, we assess and decide how to call things off, if we haven't already outlined our divorce plans somewhere along the way."

"That's more than fair." Despite not liking how clinical it sounded, Micah was impressed. Jacinta was seeing their marriage for the business arrangement it was. The fact that he had gotten a huge rush of pleasure when she'd agreed to marry him was irrelevant. He got the same heady sensation when completing any deal and refused to entertain that her acceptance might have felt slightly different. As if he'd been holding his breath until she said yes. If she'd refused his proposal, life would have proceeded as normal. Nothing would have changed. Then why this strange sense of relief and excitement and eager anticipation that she'd spend the next year under his roof? That he'd take her everywhere and introduce her as his wife?

"I do have some questions," Jacinta said, and Micah snapped back to attention. "We've said no physical intercourse. But what about other physical aspects? Abuela will not be satisfied with a mere kiss on the cheek. She'll expect us to hold hands or for you to put your arm around me. We're trying to convince her that we're madly in love, that we had this simmering tension between us for months and succumbed to an office romance. If we don't touch, we're not going convince anyone."

He had considered that aspect but had glossed over the idea lest his lust for her surface. "I'm assuming my family will want to see the same. I'm all about asking for a woman's consent, so perhaps you and I should figure out what level of physical touch we want. I'd assume handholding, and I'm fine with putting my arm around you, if that's acceptable. I don't want you uncomfortable."

Jacinta nodded. "Both those should be fine. We're going to have to kiss as well."

She didn't appear excited by the prospect and that bothered Micah greatly. "I envisioned our marriage to be a quick ceremony with a justice of the peace. We can tell our families we eloped. That will negate the kissing aspect at the wedding."

"The moment we go public, kissing will be the expectation. My grandmother will be suspicious if we don't." Jacinta's top teeth worried her lower lip.

Since she didn't appear too happy about kissing him, Micah was glad he hadn't acted on his impulses the other day at his house. When she'd been in his arms, he wouldn't have resisted if she'd made a move. Now he knew he'd misread the situation. She hadn't been into the moment. The fact bothered him more than he cared to admit.

They began to eat, letting a natural silence fall as each consumed their meal.

Micah waited until he was finished before broaching the topic again. "Should we tell Rosa we're engaged? Or should we just elope and tell her afterward? I'm fine with her being there at the justice of peace so we can swap paperwork, our license for the ownership transfer. However,

I don't want her adding any more conditions to the sale. I also don't want her to demand we kiss, especially if that's not what you want."

Jacinta's eyes widened. "I didn't say I didn't want to kiss you. I simply wanted to be sure we were on the same page. It's one thing to pretend. It's another when we're play-acting and sticking our tongues down each other's throats."

His groin tightened. His mouth would love to get to know hers better. His voice came out strangled. "You make a good point."

She moved her napkin from her lap to the box. "If we do this, I'd like us to practice kissing at least once so we're prepared. That way our first time is not in front of people who will be watching to see if we're faking. That sounds clinical, I know."

He noted that she licked her lower lip, showing she wasn't as immune to him as he might have thought. "It's a good idea. We don't want to suddenly freeze or be tense when everyone's watching. Shall we try it now? Get our first kiss over with?"

"Uh, sure?" As if Jacinta's confidence had wavered, she fingered the fabric of her cardigan like a lifeline. "There were red onions in my salad. Can I use the restroom first and freshen up?"

Micah knew this entire situation was awkward. She had to kiss her boss. He tried to put her at ease. "Of course. You don't even need to ask. How about I throw away our trash and you go prepare or do whatever you need. We'll kiss and that'll be that."

She was going to kiss Micah. *Her boss.* She'd have to step into his arms and then put her lips to his. In the privacy of the bathroom, Jacinta inspected her teeth and chewed two breath mints into oblivion before cupping her hands under the tap for a sip of water. She rinsed, spit and stuck one more mint on her tongue. Then she wiped her lips to ensure they weren't wet or covered with lipstick. Last thing she wanted was to leave Micah smeared with the bright red color she'd worn to work.

She gripped the edge of the sink before loosening her fingers and washing her hands one more time. Once dry, she smoothed out her skirt. She'd worn her favorite separates today, which were a black pencil skirt and dainty floral sweater set. Jacinta touched the small butterfly charm she wore on the end of a thin gold chain. She could do this. She could kiss Micah. She'd dreamed of it ever since that day at his house. Would the reality be better than the fantasy? She hoped it was.

Drawing in a quavering breath, she left the restroom on coltlike legs and wobbled back to the office. No one glanced her direction, which provided some sense of relief. When she closed the door behind her, though, the lock mechanism made an ominous click.

Micah arched a quizzical brow. "You look like you're walking to the gallows. Is the idea of kissing me that repugnant? Because if it is, we can call this whole thing off—"

"I'm just nervous, which is one reason I locked the door." Her stomach did a summersault. He was so handsome and she wanted him so much, but she couldn't let him know that.

"Smart. We don't want to be interrupted." He stepped toward her. "I'm nervous, too. I've never been in this situation before either."

"I'll try not to appear like I'm a virgin about to be sacrificed." Although she felt like one. Micah was a god among men. His being a great boss, fabulous mentor, and his agreement to marry her proved that.

Micah chuckled low. "I hope it won't be a sacrifice each time you have to kiss me."

Jacinta found some courage. "I'll make sure of it." She closed the gap. She'd worn lower heels so he had obvious height on her. "Although I may have to go up on tiptoe."

"I bend well. I'm going to touch you now." Her breath held as he rounded one arm around her waist. She swore her heart missed a beat as both arms encircled her. His touch created anticipatory shivers. Her face heated as he moved one hand to her jaw. "You're so pretty."

"Flatterer," she managed as her heart went from zero to sixty.

"It's the truth." One arm loosened and a thumb swooped across the corner of her mouth. "You have these perfectly shaped full lips. Like a beautiful bow waiting to be unwrapped."

She reached for the butterfly near her throat, as if doing so would calm the ones flittering in her stomach. When her lips parted by their own volition, Micah used the opportunity to run his thumb along the entirety of her bottom lip. "Beautiful," he repeated, and then he lowered his mouth to hers.

When her friends asked her later about first contact, Jacinta would tell them she'd never felt anything so wondrous. The lightest, most tentative of touches sent waves of pleasure washing over her. He tasted gently and, if it wasn't for the explosion ignited by his lips on hers, she would have described the kiss as chaste. The kiss lasted mere seconds before Micah drew back. He caught her gaze and she noted his eyes seemed as wide as hers felt. Then, without even contemplating what possessed her, much less what she was doing, Jacinta reached her hand behind his neck and pulled his head back to hers.

Kissing him was as heady as sipping fine wine. He tasted of mint and musk and male, and she drank deeply. Her tongue danced with his. Micah edged her closer. The kiss took on a life of its own, with both of them devouring each other like an unquenchable thirst. Passion flared and Micah's hands slid beyond her waist to cup her bottom. He pressed her into the part of him straining to be free. Womanly power rushed through her veins, heating her skin and activating every nerve ending. This was a kiss unlike anything she'd ever experienced before—Micah's tongue doing things inside her mouth that drove her wild. If kissing was a slate, he'd wiped it clean, branding her as his with one powerful and potent touch. How would she ever top this? She threaded her hands into his hair, her fingers memorizing the soft texture. She wanted more, and she clutched him as her own desire pulsed, keeping time with his.

Time. Oh lord. Not only had she lost track of time, she'd lost track of where they were. Jacinta's brain switched gears, focusing on the fact they were going at it in his office. She'd backed him into the dining table and he leaned against it, holding her halfway in his lap.

"Micah," she gasped. Her speaking his name acted as a cold shower for them both. He set her away from him and straightened.

"I'm sorry," he said. "I got carried away. I don't think we'll need to worry about the kissing part."

"No." She willed her heart to calm down. "That was…" She struggled for the words. "Well done."

She planted her palm over her mouth and cringed. A dark golden-blond brow arched and he laughed. "'Well done'? Am I a steak?" She noted his fingers trembled slightly as he wiped the corner of her lip. "I'd say that kiss was record-breaking. Phenomenal. Everything I'd dreamed it would be."

He'd *dreamed* of kissing her? The thought boggled and she worked for a semblance of control. If not, the implications of their lip-lock would make her wish their business relationship could be real.

"At least we know we won't have any issues convincing people." Jacinta worked to right a skirt that had slid up when she'd been pressed onto Micah's leg. "Now that we've settled that I can kiss you without dying on the sacrificial altar, I'm getting back to work."

His face remained flush as he straightened his shirt. "Sure thing. I've got some phone calls to make."

Unsure how to end this, Jacinta stuck her hand forward.

"What's this?" Micah asked wryly, taking her hand in his. Warmth fused their fingers together but Jacinta didn't pull away from his firm grip.

Instead, she gave their joined hands a little shake. "I'm finalizing our deal, especially since we can say we sealed it with a kiss. Thank you for your proposal, Micah. I accept. We're officially engaged."

Chapter Seven

Micah didn't feel like an engaged man. After a kiss that rocked his world on its axis, he and Jacinta settled right back into being platonic, business-minded coworkers for the next two days. They'd had one clinical discussion about how to best announce the engagement and what plans they should make for the ceremony. Despite knowing her as well as he did, the practicality of the discussion felt surreal. But that was what he'd suggested, right?

The two of them had settled on a semipublic display Saturday night during the dinner with Alan Bess. Micah found the venue acceptable as they were eating at Captain's, the five-star seafood restaurant on the penthouse level of the Emerald Ridge Hotel. While the place had no dress code, most of the clientele dressed to the nines, befitting the excellent food. Their table would have a fantastic view from the floor-to-ceiling windows.

But as for how to propose? Jacinta had punted that decision to him. She'd said that it was best for her to be surprised, as that would make her reaction more authentic as she insisted she was a terrible actress.

Micah had done some research, made some calls and made an after-hours stop at the local jewelry store to pick up the ring he'd ordered. When he stepped into his parents' house for a Friday-night gathering, the box had been burning a hole in his pocket.

He didn't have an excuse not to attend. Besides, since his entire family would be present, it would be the perfect time to pitch the idea of serving Abuela Rosa Chocolates to the Fortune's Gold Ranch and Spa guests. When he reached the great room, though, he discovered his father and Uncle Garth commanding everyone's attention with a discussion of ranch operations and sabotage updates.

"I'm still going undercover," he said as he accepted a drink. "The last of my disguise finally arrives Saturday. At this point, I should have gone into Dallas for it, but I don't think they would have had what I wanted. It's coming from a Hollywood props department and was custom made for me."

"I still think that's a good plan," his dad said. "While things have been mostly quiet here, other ranches in the area are still having issues. We know someone on our ranch knows something, but it's been impossible to figure out. Vivienne, you were telling us about—"

The shrilling of the doorbell interrupted their conversation. Micah's frown joined those of the others. Everyone in the family was in the room, including his cousins' significant others. The way the ranch was set up, a stranger simply couldn't show up at the door. But it appeared as if that had happened.

"Ma'am, you can't just burst in here!" Micah heard the family butler say.

"They have my baby!" a hysterical female voice shouted. "I want my child! Give me my son!"

Micah's cousin Poppy gasped and everyone froze as a late-twenties woman burst into the room. For someone who'd recently given birth, she was tall and fit. Dressed in blue jeans and a T-shirt, the woman's brown-eyed gaze darted over the room, searching each of the Fortunes' shocked expressions. "Where's my child? I want him back!"

"Sir, I tried to stop her. Do you want me to call security?" The butler appeared frazzled.

Garth spoke first. "Not yet." He faced the woman. "Who are you?"

Her chin jutted forward and her chest heaved. "I'm the baby's mother. I want my child. He's mine. Not yours."

Leo, Poppy's fiancé, took charge. "I understand you're upset, ma'am, but Joey is in foster care. There are legal processes that have to take place first. You can't just take him."

"I don't care. He's mine." She glanced around, and seeing a bassinet in the corner, rushed over. Micah, being closest, moved to block her. "Joey," the woman wailed, finding herself thwarted. She cried huge, fat tears. She seemed almost as if she were acting, if he was being honest. And badly.

"Don't," he warned her, his tone firm as she made to move around. "Joey is sleeping and we're not going to bother him."

Micah saw something shift in her brown eyes. Still crying and sniffing her nose, she stepped back a pace and shoved her light brown hair behind her ear. "You aren't being fair. You can't keep him."

"Since we have no idea who are you, I'd say we're being more than fair. Who do you think you are, rushing in here like this?" Micah chastised.

Over the woman's head, he could see Leo pull an emotional Poppy into his arms. Leo planted a kiss on her forehead. "Who are you anyway?" Micah demanded.

The woman found her footing and jutted her chin forward. "I'm Jennifer Johnson and I'm the baby's mother."

"Prove it." Micah leveled the challenge in two words.

More hair went behind her ear, revealing multiple silver piercings. "He looks like me."

"Babies' eyes can change," Micah's mom said. Around the room, various family members had recovered from their shock and begun shifting about.

"I'll take a DNA test. Let's go right now," Jennifer demanded.

"The labs are closed," Garth said. "Even for people like us."

"You mean Fortunes," the woman snarled.

Micah heard the hate in Jennifer's tone and had to contain himself as to not snap back. "Yes, the very people on whose doorstep you claim you dropped your baby," Micah said calmly. "The ones who could be calling the police right now but for some reason haven't while we give you the benefit of the doubt."

"Why *did* you leave your baby with us?" Poppy demanded. Micah was glad to see his cousin had found her voice, the one that made her so formidable in business. "What kind of a mother are you to leave a child on our doorstep?"

"I needed help and you all have everything. I wanted my baby to be raised with everything I can't give it." Jennifer added more exaggerated tears and sniffles.

"There are programs for that," Poppy said. Micah noted his cousin's sympathy stretched only so far for Joey's alleged mom.

Jennifer appeared agitated and her voice grew angry. "Are there really? You're a foster mom. You know how not everyone is the best person for their child. You also know that the system favors the mother. I will get him back. He's mine!"

"He's currently a ward of the court," Poppy said firmly. As Joey began to fuss, she went to the bassinet and lifted him. She swaddled Joey in a blue blanket covered with bunnies and he quieted. He nestled his head onto Poppy's shoulder. "You'll need to deal with the judge first. I'm sure he'll want a DNA test. Then the judge will decide what to do."

Jennifer's haughty head toss made Micah dislike her even more. "Fine. I'll provide one. I'll go first thing tomorrow."

"Good." Poppy stroked Joey's back, her fingers moving in a rhythmical fashion. "Because I'm not giving him up otherwise."

Jennifer's face morphed from sadness to anger to resignation. "Maybe you should keep him. It's clear you've bonded. I'll relinquish my rights for half a million dollars."

Micah's family, spectators since the drama had started, collectively gasped. His mother's fingers flew to her lips. Poppy's eyes widened, and Micah knew she was as horrified as he was that Jennifer could be a grifter.

"You'd sell your child? You've already left him once. You don't deserve him," Poppy criticized. She drew Joey closer and pivoted so Jennifer got a view of her shoulder and not the baby. "What kind of a mother are you?"

"Not as good of one as you'll be." Jennifer's tears began to flow and her shoulders shook as she sobbed. "I need a fresh start. You can afford it. We can do the DNA test and I'll sign over my rights for the cash."

Leo had moved protectively in front of Poppy and Joey. "We need to discuss this. Leave your contact information and we can go to the lab on Monday. It's closed for the weekend."

Micah, anticipating this, had retrieved a pen and a pad of paper from the shelf next to the collection of board games. "Here." He thrust the items into Jennifer's hands. The woman scribbled down a number and he took it from her. "I'll walk you out."

"I'm not a bad person," she said as they walked toward the front door. "I want what's best for the baby."

Micah, who sincerely doubted that, said nothing.

As Jennifer walked outside, a gust of wind blew and he stepped back. He noted she drove a dusty, older model sedan, but as her tires squealed, he couldn't see her license plate number, which had been shoved into the back window instead of being properly mounted on the bumper. He found the family having an intense discussion when he returned.

"I don't believe she's the mother," Shane said. "She's not a physical match for the woman who tried to kidnap Joey last month while I was babysitting. She was shorter and slight. I could tell that even though she was fully disguised. It can't be her."

"Maybe the kidnapper was the real mother. Maybe she'd had a change of heart and came back for him," Vivienne mused.

"What if the kidnapper was instead an opportunist hoping for a big payout?" Garth countered. "We have to consider that angle as well."

"Yeah, along with the fact we may have just met Joey's real mom," Rafe added.

Micah shook his head. "My gut doesn't think Jennifer will be the mother. She's too slick. Those tears were faked."

"Well, in any case, Poppy, Leo, you should call the police and report this."

"If we'd been thinking, we should have called them while she was here instead of giving her the benefit of the doubt and talking to her," Rafe said. "Abandoning the child is a crime. They could have arrested her and gotten the DNA."

"Well, we were too shocked and trying to do the right thing," Micah's mom reminded him. "I still can't believe she stormed in here. And then when she demanded money."

"We have her phone number. We'll get her to take a DNA test and go from there," Garth said. "We have Joey's DNA, so we should be able to know conclusively if she is or isn't the mother."

"I don't even want to think about her as Joey's mother," Poppy huffed.

"I'm trying to find her online now," Rafe said, his fingers on his phone. "But there are tons of Jennifer Johnsons. It's a common name. If that even *is* her name."

"We can't pay some opportunist a half a million dollars," Micah's dad interjected. "If we do, they'll come out of the woodwork presenting us with babies. Last thing we need is to be accused like Garth was."

Poppy and Leo had been talking quietly while conversation went on around them. "Leo and I will meet with the police tomorrow and discuss how to handle this," Poppy said. "Until then, I'm taking Joey home and putting him to bed."

Given the circumstances, Micah decided his pitching Jacinta's chocolates could keep. The entire family had had enough drama for the night. As for his impending nuptials, they'd find out tomorrow anyway, after the reveal.

"Are you ready for tonight?"

The sound of Micah's voice jolted Jacinta from staring at her computer. Normally, she could hear him approach, but she'd been so deep in thought that she'd missed the tell-tale noises, like the soft click of his office door opening or his firm footfalls on the carpet. Perhaps that was because they were working a rare Saturday afternoon trying to get everything finished as she officially exited her role as Micah's admin.

Monday, she'd move to another part of the office, working with the salesforce. A cardboard box containing her possessions sat on her desk. Yesterday morning, she'd met with her replacement, an MBA student graduating a year behind her. Jacinta had liked the man's work enthusiasm. With previous experience and a willingness to ask questions, she expected he'd adjust to Micah's managerial style.

"I have to change my clothes, but otherwise, I'm good." Strange to think of Micah as her fiancé. Their relationship was strictly a business deal.

Right?

He leaned his hip against her desk, which lowered him slightly. Still, he loomed larger than life. "Last chance to back out."

"No. I'm not changing my mind. I'm in." After that kiss, how could she not be? The kiss had stolen her breath and weakened her knees. She'd wanted to cling to him and prolong the moment. Last night, she'd also had a long conversation with her girlfriends, swearing them to secrecy. Her friends found the idea of marrying Micah brilliant.

"You should leave. Go and get ready. I'll pick you up later," he told her.

"I wasn't sure how long we'd work. My things are here…" She'd also avoided telling her grandmother where she was going or who with.

"You can use my private bathroom to change," Micah suggested. He glanced at his watch. "Better yet, leave with me and dress at my house. Move that box to your new desk and we'll go in ten minutes. Sound good?"

"Of course." A steadying breath calmed her stomach gymnastics. Soon it would be her home, too. But parts of Micah's offer made her worry she was a gold digger, especially the monthly allowance he'd set. Perhaps if they loved each other it would be different, but this was a business deal with mutual benefits. Sure, her high school world history class had been filled with royal marriages based on nothing but strategic alliances, but that didn't mean Jacinta had warmed to the idea of a marriage of convenience, even if Micah was the sexiest man she'd ever met whose mere presence curled her toes. Already she felt things for him she shouldn't, and that earth-shattering kiss lived large in her head.

"You ready?" the man in question asked.

This time, attuned to the passing minutes, she'd heard him coming. Monday, she'd be the subject of gossip and speculation, so to divert herself, she blared the radio as she followed behind his crossover. He drove in a back entrance, showing Jacinta a shortcut. Since he owned two vehicles, she figured it would be safe to park in front of the fourth-car garage bay.

Micah met her as she stepped out of her car. "I'll get you a remote so you can keep your car in this part of the garage." He gazed at her late-model sedan. "Better yet, you need a new car." The words "not in my budget" died on her tongue as he continued. "One worthy of my wife. I'll arrange it."

Figuring she'd argue later that the allowance he was insisting on could cover a car payment, she followed him through the garage. He led her up the back staircase to the second floor. "There are four bedrooms," he said. "This is my suite, and I converted the other bedroom in this wing into a home gym."

She gave a quick glance into his bedroom, catching sight of a dark wood, king-sized bedframe with a tufted brown-leather headboard. A thick, woven, paisley comforter in tan, brown and caramel colors was complemented with patches of distressed leather accents. They crossed the bridge that overlooked the foyer and the great room, entering opposite.

"Both of these bedrooms have en suite bathrooms. The

HVAC is on its own zone, so you can control the temperature."

He pushed open the door to a bedroom. "This one has a better view. Feel free to redecorate any and all rooms, including downstairs, and if you need anything, let me know. Communication is the key to a successful partnership. Let's be honest with each other at all times."

"I can do that." Jacinta stepped into a huge room with a queen-sized bed covered with a light floral quilt. The walls were a warm white, with a hint of robin's egg, and the cottage-style furniture created an airy, welcoming charm. She didn't even need to check the other bedroom, not once she glanced out the window and saw the fields beyond. Setting the bag containing her dress, shoes and makeup on the dresser, she murmured, "This bedroom is perfect."

"Great. We'll convert the other to your home office. Once you move the factory into its new location, you can work here or there." Micah remained in the doorway, as if the sexual tension between them was a force field he dare not cross. Ever since that kiss, her eyes had been drawn to him like a fork to a delectable sweet. She craved another taste, if only to prove the first delicious taste must have been a fluke.

He gestured to a door. "Bathroom is fully stocked. Come downstairs when you're ready."

"Okay. See you soon."

Micah closed the door behind him, the little click reverberating in her heart telling her that this was real. She'd be living in this beautiful room and… Her thoughts derailed as she stepped into the most gorgeous bathroom she'd ever seen. There were double sinks, a dressing table and a walk-in shower with a seat, rainfall showerhead and hand wand. If she wanted a bath, there was a whirlpool tub. The toilet had its own space behind a door. Fluffy white towels hung from decorative bars, and some designer had ensured that the liquid soap, tissue and toothbrush-holder containers matched, as did the artwork on the walls.

Overwhelmed, she retrieved her garment bag. She had about an hour and a half before it was time to leave, but it wouldn't take her that long to get ready. Jacinta removed the black cocktail dress from the protective plastic cover. Refusing Micah's credit card, she'd purchased the classic sheath at a higher end boutique in Emerald Ridge, straying slightly outside her budget. As the salesperson had said, the dress would be perfect for events like tonight and she could wear it under her graduation gown. She hung the dress in an empty walk-in closet larger than her bedroom at Abuela's.

When she finished her makeup, she stepped into the dress and drew the fabric over her shoulders. Then she did the wiggle every woman knew well, first with arms behind her waist to get the zipper up to half, and then arms reaching backward over the shoulders to pull the zipper the rest of the way. She'd worn her hair down, and her fingers fumbled with the clasp. Giving up, she slid her feet into her heels and stepped out into the hallway.

Micah was leaving his bedroom. He stopped short and turned her direction. "Wow," he said.

Jacinta touched the small silver butterfly charm. "I hope it's not too plain."

He slid a cufflink into the slot at his left wrist. "It's perfect. You look fantastic." Her cheeks warmed as he came closer. "I'll be the envy of everyone there."

Jacinta's breath caught as the tempest of desire darkening his eyes affected her more than it should. "You're bordering on overkill."

"It's the truth. Shall we?" He offered her his arm.

Boosted by her heels, she fit into Micah's side as they walked downstairs and into the kitchen. He released her to retrieve his dark blue suit jacket that lay across a barstool. Inside the pocket, she could see the outline of a small box. Butterflies in her stomach joined the one on her necklace and a lump formed in her throat. This was happening.

"By the way, tonight will go without a hitch. I've got the ring in my jacket pocket," he said. "At the right time, I'll pull it out, get on one knee and ask you. It's real proposal. It should look like one."

"Real in name only." Jacinta made to nibble her lower lip but caught herself in time before she damaged her red lipstick. "I did tell my friends. But don't worry, I swore them to secrecy. They were the ones who convinced me that marrying you wouldn't be so terrible."

Micah laughed at that. "Well, I'm not telling anyone."

"You can, as long as they won't blab. Discretion is key. We both have too much too lose."

"The only people I'd trust would be my brother and sister." He gazed at her. "Are you okay? What are you doing?"

Jacinta had reached under her hair and fingered where the dress clasp wasn't fastened. "Oh, it's just the clasp. I couldn't get it myself."

"Let me."

Jacinta used both hands to lift her hair, holding the long strands against her head. As Micah found the tiny metal hook and slid it through the corresponding metal eye, the back of his fingers brushed against her neck. The gesture wasn't intended to be intimate, but she drew in a sharp breath as goose bumps pebbled and a shiver ran down her spine.

"There." Micah's voice came out husky. "All fixed."

"Thank you." When she released her hands, her hair cascaded over her shoulders. "Shall we go? Protocol dictates that we don't want your father or Mr. Bess to arrive before we do."

"That, we don't." Micah looped his suit jacket over his arm and grabbed for the car fob. They walked out into the garage and passed the crossover. Jacinta assumed they were taking the huge truck, until Micah walked around it.

It was then she realized that there were three vehicles in the garage—the hybrid crossover, the diesel-dually crew cab and, hidden from view, a two-door sports coupe. She stopped. "That's a Maserati."

He grinned. "It's electric and does zero to sixty in 2.7 seconds. Top speed is around two hundred. Not that we'll be going anywhere close to that." He unhooked the car from the charger. "You're safe with me. Always. And I never go that fast, not unless I take her to the track."

He open the passenger door. "Slide in. It was delivered a month ago. You're the first nonfamily member who's been in it. Can't wait to know what you think."

She sat on the sumptuous leather seat and buckled in. The car cost a small fortune, but then again, he was Micah Fortune and he could afford a car that cost more than the amount she'd first offered Abuela.

The sleek sports car made no noise, minus the beeping of the backup camera. "That's the one thing that's different," Micah said. "I can't decide if I miss the purring reverberations of a sports car motor or like that I can hear nothing."

His hands gripped the leather-wrapped wheel with confidence as he maneuvered around her car parked in his driveway. "You'll have to tell me what type of car you want. One thing I insisted on was an oversized garage so whatever you choose will fit. I'll give you the garage opener when we get back."

He looked both ways and drove out onto the main road.

Then grinned. "Want to see what it can do? Within reason, of course."

His boyish excitement was contagious. "Sure."

Micah stepped on the accelerator and the g-force pushed Jacinta back against the seat as the car shot down the road like a rocket. When she laughed, he said, "I know, right? It's incredible."

As promised, Micah obeyed the speed limit, and soon they were parked and taking the elevator to the top floor of the Emerald Ridge Hotel. They'd arrived at Captain's first and waited in the bar. She savored the French 75 cocktail she'd ordered, letting the gin mixed with champagne work its bubbly magic. Micah sipped two fingers of bourbon. Then she stilled as his parents appeared in the doorway.

Micah's mom was one of those women who made dark-haired bangs and shoulder-length hair look fabulous. She wore a white silk shirt tucked into a floor-length skirt. Like Baby Bear's porridge, her outfit was perfect. Micah's father wore a suit jacket over an open-collared shirt. Like Micah, he'd gone without a tie. Both parents were in their early sixties, and Hayden had let his closely cropped beard and mustache go gray, which matched the salt-and-pepper streak he'd swooped away from his forehead. If Micah aged as well as his father, his handsome looks would never fade. She refused to imagine them old and gray together. They had a year, max.

"Jacinta," his mom greeted as she approached the high top. "How are you?"

"I'm well. Thank you for asking, Mrs. Fortune."

The rings on her fingers glittered as she waved off the formality. "Darla, dear. Micah's told us far too much about his fabulous administrative assistant for us not to be on a first-name basis."

"Today was her last day as my assistant," Micah said. "She's got an MBA, so I've found Jacinta another role and one she's better suited for."

Jacinta, midsip, coughed as the delicious cocktail went down wrong. "He means I've moved over to work with the sales team." She found her composure.

"Jacinta is also taking over Abuela Rosa Chocolates at the end of the month. The other night I meant to discuss bringing her chocolates to the guest ranch, but we were preoccupied."

"I can't believe that horrible woman actually took a DNA test. What type of person…" Darla stopped herself. "Sorry. We are not going to talk about her tonight. Tonight is about wooing Alan and his wife and having fun while we're doing it. It's been a while since I've had a night out."

Hayden's hands went up in mock surrender. "Guilty. But we do have that long vacation planned and I'm going to make it up to you."

Darla laughed and leaned conspiratorially toward her. "That's the key to a successful marriage, Jacinta. Make sure they know they have to make things up to you when they fail to live up to your expectations. Like taking me out more."

"I'm trained to know it's always my fault," Hayden joked. He slid his arm around his wife and gave her a light kiss. "Even when it's not."

"Oh, sweetie. It's *always* your fault." Darla patted his cheek lovingly before craning her head. "Mr. and Mrs. Bess are here."

With that, the groups merged. Their table-with-a-view was in a quieter part of the popular restaurant and Jacinta enjoyed the evening. Alan and Marie were delightful people, and Darla knew how to keep an easy, friendly conversation going. No business was discussed, as that would occur later at the meeting Jacinta had added to the calendar as one of her last duties.

After he and Jacinta ordered dessert, Micah whispered in her ear. "Ready?"

A brief panic seized her. Calming herself, she nodded. Micah waited until their server finished taking the rest of the dessert orders before he caught the attention of the table. "Remember how I told you I had another role in mind for Jacinta?"

Four heads swiveled their direction. "You mentioned her MBA," Hayden said.

"This one's more personal." Micah scooted his chair back and, like magic, a small black jewelry box appeared in his hand. "Jacinta, I'm not exactly down on one knee, but you've already knocked me for a loop in the short time we've known each other. Will you marry me?"

With that, he lifted the lid and Jacinta's gasp joined that of his mother and Marie Bess as Jacinta stared at the most gorgeous ring she'd ever seen. Micah hadn't gone for a traditional diamond, nor an ostentatious engagement ring. A princess-cut center stone was surrounded by two smaller stones, both emeralds. The center stone appeared almost as if it was red, but it wasn't, Jacinta noted. She held out her hand.

"I take it that's a yes?" Micah teased.

"Yes," she whispered, wishing this moment was real. Instead, it was surreal as Micah shifted so he could hold her hand.

"That's a beautiful ring," his mother said, trying to hide her shock. "What's the stone?"

"Alexandrite." Micah slid the ring onto her finger, his flesh warm against hers. "It's a combination of iron, titanium and chromium. The jeweler described the gem as an emerald by day and ruby by night. I wanted something as unique as Jacinta. Especially since this has been such a whirlwind romance."

"Obviously, as none of us had any idea." His father frowned. "You could have said something the other night when I was rambling on."

Micah kept his hands on Jacinta's. "I was her mentor. We had to keep things quiet until my part of her course-work was done. But the feeling was always there, wasn't it, honey?"

His use of an endearment threw her, but Jacinta managed a happy smile. Micah leaned closer and dropped a light kiss on her lips. Her mouth tingled and immediately missed his touch.

"This calls for champagne!" his mother exclaimed, motioning the server over. "I'm so thrilled. Have you told anyone?"

"You're the first to know."

That made his mother smile even more. "Why, we'll have to start planning. There are so many details. Have you set a date?"

"Soon. Before the end of the month. Maybe just the courthouse. I don't want to waste any more time," Micah said.

"No." This came from his father. "No son of mine is doing some quick courthouse wedding like she's pregnant."

"Which I'm *not*," Jacinta inserted. She hadn't even had sex with Micah, although after the two kisses and the way his hand rested on her knee, the idea held great appeal.

"We don't want to have a long engagement," Micah said. "When you know, you know. We're telling her family tomorrow. Afterward, I'll swing by the ranch. Until we tell her grandmother, can we keep this under wraps? Minus everyone who just saw us."

"Certainly," Hayden said. Jacinta had the impression Micah's dad had tons of questions. But the server brought the champagne and desserts, and Darla soon had Alan and Marie telling everyone about how they'd fallen in love, taking the pressure off the two of them.

Jacinta was grateful for the distraction. Now that they were officially engaged, Micah kept his hand on her upper thigh. He touched her as often as possible, as a loving fiancé would, draping his arm across the back of her chair while everyone lingered over coffee.

When dinner ended, Darla drew Jacinta into her arms and said, "Can't wait to chat wedding plans."

Hayden clapped Micah on the back and told him, "Proud of you, son."

Jacinta leaned against the Maserati seat as Micah pulled slowly away from the curb. "That went well," he said.

"It did." The radio made soft background noise. "Admittedly sort of dreamlike. It's a lovely ring."

"I'm glad you like it. I saw the stone the other day and thought of you. The jeweler told me he had the perfect setting, and he was right."

The fact the jeweler had dropped everything to customize a ring again showed the power of being Micah Fortune. Once parked in his garage, Jacinta slid from car before he could open her door. "I'll grab my stuff."

"Stay for a bit," he said as they reached the kitchen. Stepping toward her, he gently tucked some of her hair behind her ear. "Let's watch a movie or something."

"I…" She couldn't find an excuse to go home. What she wanted was to be in his arms, have his lips on hers. He read her mind, for his face eased closer, and then she closed her eyes and let herself feel the way Micah's mouth worked its magic. A fire began to burn, making Jacinta clutch his forearms. Her tongue danced against his, and tingles coursed through her as Micah moved his hand to the back of her neck, deepening the kiss.

Then a coolness descended as he stepped away. "Maybe it's best if we don't watch a movie," he said thickly. "I'm finding myself losing control, so if you don't go grab your things…" He let the rest go unsaid.

Jacinta knew he wouldn't pressure her to do anything. But tonight, as intoxicating as the thought of making Micah lose control by making love to him sounded, their relationship was complicated enough.

"Rain check," Jacinta managed to say as she headed upstairs. Then she realized she couldn't get herself out of the dress. Remembering how Micah's fingers had felt against her skin and not trusting herself to say no, she kept the dress on and packed. Once she'd finished, she found Micah at the bottom of the stairs. He handed her the ring box and she dropped it in her purse. "Are you good to drive?"

The meal had lasted almost four hours and she'd skipped the wine. The French 75 and a sip of champagne had been all she'd had. "Yes."

He walked her out the front door to her car and opened the door. "Text me when you get home?"

"I will," Jacinta promised. He leaned down and satisfied himself with seeing she'd buckled herself in.

He dropped a light kiss on her lips. "Thank you."

"For what?" Her car's engine sputtered before it roared to life.

He glanced at the hood but spared her the criticism. "Thank you for a wonderful evening. For agreeing to marry me. For being you. I'm looking forward to tomorrow."

She liked Micah and enjoyed spending time with him. "Me, too."

"We're going to get everything we want," he promised, misinterpreting her agreement. "Don't forget to text me and sleep well."

He stood in the driveway until she could no longer see him. Jacinta opened the window to let in the cooler night air. She turned up the radio, singing along as the band Joy-wave filled the car. When she got home, she slid the ring from her finger and put it safely in the box. Then she entered the darkened house. While it wasn't even ten thirty, Abuela was in bed and hadn't waited up.

Jacinta closed her bedroom door and set the bag down. She slid the ring back onto her finger. Holding her hand aloft, she studied the ring and its implications. How she wished this were real, that her life was different and she didn't need to resort to these methods to get her grandmother's company.

She was falling for Micah. How could she *not*? He was perfect. Handsome. Thoughtful. Kind. Caring. The list went on and on. He kissed divine. If he hadn't stepped back, the night would have ended in his bed. But Micah didn't love her.

We're going to get everything we want, he'd said.

As Jacinta tucked the ring away, she faced a hard truth. She was forgoing her prospects for finding love, at least for a year. What she really wanted, she couldn't have. Would never have.

Even if she was Mrs. Micah Fortune.

Chapter Eight

Abuela didn't usually work on Sundays, but since a Mother's Day rush order had arrived from an old friend who owned two flower shops, Jacinta found herself making chocolate with her grandmother and cousin. Sofia, of course, had miraculously discovered an interest in a business Jacinta knew she planned to dump as soon as the ink dried on the transfer paperwork.

Not going to happen, cousin. Jacinta allowed herself a secretive smile.

"What's got you in such a good mood?" Sofia asked.

Jacinta wiped the smile from her face. "Nothing."

Her hands covered in food-grade gloves, Sofia packaged the finished heart-shaped chocolates, placing them in small paper cubes decorated with hearts. They needed two hundred of them as the client planned to attach them to her Mother's Day bouquets that would be delivered midweek. To be efficient, Abuela was making an additional three hundred for other clients.

Her cousin peered at Jacinta. "If I didn't know any better, I'd say you got some action last night."

"Sofia!" Abuela rebuked sharply.

"What?" Sofia protested. After dropping another chocolate into the box, she gestured toward Jacinta. "Seriously.

Look at her. It's like she's glowing. And I said action, not sex."

Abuela huffed at her granddaughter's behavior but said nothing.

"Who is he?" Sofia persisted.

Jacinta moved boxes filled with the chocolates over to another area.

"You were out late," Abuela acknowledged as she went by.

"I had a work dinner. I told you that," Jacinta said. "I was home by ten thirty. You went to bed early."

Rosa waved a chocolate-covered finger. She'd been painting designs on some of the candy bars and the end of her glove had paid the price. "Work, work. All you do."

"Clearly, as I'm here today." Jacinta grumbled as she grabbed some additional packaging.

"Yes, Jacinta, how will you find a husband if you don't do anything but work?" Sofia tossed aside one of the paper boxes that had ripped and Jacinta made a mental note to check on the suppliers for their packaging. While some loss was to be expected, it seemed Sofia had destroyed more than an inordinate number, as if something frustrated her. Her cousin seemed more agitated than normal.

Jacinta decided to wade into the skirmish. "I will have no problem finding a husband."

"You married in three weeks?" Sofia's scoff indicated her disbelief.

Jacinta drew on some gloves and began filling individual boxes. "Takes but a trip to Vegas."

The other woman paused. Then she laughed. "I can see you going to Vegas on the thirty-first and begging someone to marry you."

"As if," Jacinta shot back. "I'm not desperate."

"Girls. Be nice," Abuela admonished before she went to check on the double chocolate truffles whose outer coatings should have set.

Sofia lowered her voice. "Life isn't a movie, Jacinta. No white knight is riding to your rescue. Face it, you've lost. This place is going to be mine."

"Never," Jacinta hissed back.

"Please." Sofia drew out the word. "You might have gotten a little something something last night but sex doesn't equate to love and marriage. Marriage is hard work, and the only work you can manage is getting your MBA."

"At least I have one," Jacinta shot back, her tolerance threshold breached.

"That may be true, but no degree will save this business. I run a successful one and can tell you an MBA is a piece of paper you hang on a wall. It doesn't mean you'll succeed. You've focused on the wrong things." She smirked. "But at least you're getting your needs met by someone. That way you won't be lonely when this goes bye-bye."

Jacinta tucked both of her lips under, thinning her mouth into a tight line. Abuela had always stressed that when you didn't have anything good to say, you didn't say anything, a lesson Sofia had clearly missed. "You know, Sofia, I do have something. In fact, I have an announcement. Abuela? You should hear this, too."

"You're finally going to give up and let this go, aren't you?" Sofia appeared smug.

"No, I'm not. And you—" she directed this at her cousin "—should stop needling me."

Abuela walked toward the two girls, her apron criss-crossed with lines of red and white chocolate. "Stop bickering. I made my decision. Jacinta has until the end of the month. You—" she looked directly at Sofia "—should be more gracious. You're family."

"She's just upset this will be mine." Sofia gave an apologetic pout.

"She's angry because I told her it wouldn't be." Jacinta stopped herself from sneering. "What I didn't say was I got engaged last night."

The shop became so silent, Jacinta swore she could hear the proverbial pin drop. Then Sofia burst out laughing. "Oh *please*. That's a good one."

Jacinta stood firm. "The ring is in the house. Would you like to see it?"

"You're not even dating. How can you be engaged?" Sofia protested. "Abuela, this has to simply be for convenience." She eyed Jacinta skeptically. "All you've done is work. Where would you have met someone?"

"Work," Jacinta answered, sticking with the truth. "We had to keep it quiet because it could have been seen as a conflict of interest. But, as of yesterday, my internship is over. He completed my performance review days ago."

Sofia's jaw had loosened and her mouth dropped open. "Are you saying that—"

"I'm marrying Micah Fortune," Jacinta confirmed. "He proposed to me last night at Captain's, in front of his parents. I hope that's official enough for you."

Abuela recovered first and gave Jacinta a huge hug. "*¡Mi querida nieta!* I am so happy!"

Jacinta managed not to wince after being called "beloved granddaughter." This wasn't a love match. "Thank you. I'll show you the ring after we finish here. It's lovely. He outdid himself." Micah had. She loved the ring. She just couldn't let herself fall all the way in love with him. As it was, with him the door to her heart had cracked wide open.

"Congrats," Sofia said. Jacinta heard the envy her cousin tried to mask with begrudging surprise. "Micah Fortune. I guessed there was something going on between you two when I saw you at the restaurant."

"Perhaps." Jacinta knew the less she said, the better.

"He's a nice man," Abuela said. "He'll come for dinner?"

"I'll text him." Since they had planned to tell their respective families together, she needed to give him a heads-up anyway that she'd let her family know. "I'd prefer we don't make a big deal out of this. We'd like to keep it to ourselves until Micah and I tell the rest of his family." She glanced at Sofia. "Can you do that?"

"Of course she will," Abuela said. "We all will. I'll set another place for dinner."

"I'll ask him. He had some business at the ranch."

"He'll come. Now, shall we finish?" With that, Abuela left her granddaughters to continue boxing the chocolates.

"I can't believe you're marrying Micah Fortune," Sofia hissed a few minutes later once Abuela was out of earshot. "No wonder why you were on cloud nine earlier. You're marrying one of the town's most eligible bachelors."

"Yes. Yes, I am." Jacinta allowed herself one second of a satisfied smile. Would Sofia have been so envious if it had been just anyone? Probably not.

"Then this will be yours and I hope you'll be happy." Sofia sighed. "I do mean that."

"Thank you," Jacinta said. With the exception of the love her grandmother had expected her to find, she finally had everything she wanted within her grasp,

While Jacinta was boxing chocolates, Micah sat in the ranch office, interviewing for a spot as a gig worker on his family's ranch. From the end of a small conference table, he faced both his brother, Drake, and his sister, Vivienne, and two ranch managers who reported directly to Vivienne. Both men had grilled him nonstop, questioning everything from how he spotted sick cattle to how he took care of horse tack.

"Is there anything else you need to tell us, Toby?" Vivienne asked. Only Micah saw the twinkle in her eye. Otherwise, she'd remained in character, not indicating she knew Toby was her brother in disguise.

"My résumé shows I've been roping and riding most of my life," Micah answered. It wasn't a lie. He'd been seated on a saddle almost as soon as he could walk, same as the rest of his siblings. "I won't let you down."

"I will, of course, be checking your references," his sister said. "And these men here will be reporting to me if you can't do the job you've assured me you can do."

"Yes, ma'am. I understand."

"Good," Vivienne said. She turned to her employees. "You two may go. I have more questions for Toby, but I've got it from here. I'm expecting his references to check out, so plan for him to bring his gear tomorrow and start Tuesday morning."

After their nods, Micah watched the men shuffle out. Drake stood, peered out into the hallway and locked the conference room door.

"I think they bought it," Micah said. His disguise was good. He wore a dark-haired wig, a prosthetic nose and thick black mustache, colored contacts and utilitarian ranch clothing. His boots and hat were of higher quality but similar to what most of the ranch workers wore, and both items were creased with dirt and wear. He wouldn't stand out as a newbie who didn't have a clue.

"Yeah, they bought it, cuz you sure don't look anything

like this guy. Care to tell us what's going on?" Drake turned his phone toward Micah. The image onscreen was a social media post of Micah sliding an engagement ring on Jacinta's finger. "How did we not know you were even dating the girl?"

"A congrats would be in order," Micah said, picking at the grit under his fingernails.

His brother tapped his forefinger on the table. "I would give you one, if I believed this was real. You swore up and down you would never get engaged. Especially after being cheated on. Yet here you are, in public with our parents, putting a ring on it."

"Jacinta's different. We had to keep it quiet."

Vivienne leaned forward. "This is *us*, Micah. You forget we know you. We might be lying to find the saboteur, but don't lie to us. What's really going on?"

Micah hesitated for only a moment. "Jacinta was going to lose everything, including the chocolate business her grandmother started, unless she married by the end of the month."

"And you volunteered." This surprised statement came from Drake.

Micah nodded. "I did. There's no way I'm getting emotionally involved with a woman for a long time, maybe ever. Jacinta understands that."

"Huh." His sister leaned back and studied him. "And what do you get out of it, minus a woman who's beautiful and younger than you?"

He tried for a nonchalant approach. "You heard our father. He thinks it's unnatural that a man of my age is not married. He thinks it hinders business deals as men think I'm after their wives or girlfriends who see me as available or something. You get that, right, Drake?" His brother was often confused for the actor Chris Hemsworth and women found the younger Fortune incredibly sexy.

"I don't get that," Drake said. "I mean the 'getting hit on' part, yeah. But it's never been an issue."

"Maybe because you're not CEO," Micah suggested wryly. "Anyway, she needed a husband and I figured why not enter into a marriage of convenience and have a wife? It was a win-win for us both."

"This isn't a love match?" Vivienne's gaze narrowed in that disapproving way that reminded Micah of his mother.

"No, and you can't reveal that. I'm confiding in both of you, but you'll ruin this for Jacinta and me if you tell anyone. I told her I trusted you two."

"We will keep your secret," Drake assured him. "We're already keeping one, what's another? But this isn't like you. It's out of character. You've known her what? Since January?"

Another nod and the wig remained put, making it worth what he'd spent. "She's been the best administrative assistant I've ever had, and I don't want her dreams snatched away from her by an old-fashioned grandmother who is insisting she marry or lose everything she's worked for."

"Uh-huh." Drake clearly didn't believe him. "Yeah, you're a softie, but not that much of one. Not enough to marry someone you hardly know, even if you did work with her daily for several months."

"Well, it is what it is. We'll be here for dessert tonight. We have to go visit her grandmother first. We were planning something small at the courthouse—" he ignored his sister's gasp "—but dad said no to that idea."

"As he should! Micah, you're such a dunce." Vivienne tossed a pen at him, which he caught one-handed.

Micah's phone chimed. Setting the pen down, he read the

text. Jacinta had apologized and said she'd told her family. "I need to go get changed out of this getup, so, if there's nothing else?" He gazed pointedly at each of his siblings.

"No," Vivienne said. Drake simply shook his head.

"See you tonight." Micah went outside and climbed into an old, beat-up pickup he'd secured for his undercover persona. He drove it out the ranch gates, and then, after taking different roads to ensure he wasn't followed, he drove back to his house and parked the truck in the empty bay. After peeling off his disguise, he showered and changed, and drove the crossover to Jacinta's. As he pulled into the driveway, he sent her a text saying he'd arrived.

Let the masquerade begin.

Jacinta held the screen door open for Micah as he stepped onto the porch. "Hey," she said.

"Hey," he replied, drawing her into his arms and lowering his head for kiss that didn't end until the screen door slammed behind them. Jacinta jumped at the sound.

"Aren't you both so adorable," Sofia said. She watched from the doorway and reopened the screen door. "Micah, congratulations. I hear you're joining our family."

"I am." Micah circled his arm around Jacinta's waist. He lifted her ring finger and kissed the back of her hand, the precious stone glittering in the light. "I'm a lucky man."

"I'd say." Luis, Jacinta's uncle, came outside to shake Micah's hand. "Jacinta kept a pretty big secret."

"She had her reasons," Micah replied. "But circumstances changed, so we moved our timetable forward."

"Of course you did," Sofia said. "And with such a pretty ring, too…"

"A beautiful woman deserves a ring worthy of her."

Micah dropped another kiss on Jacinta's lips and she pressed her hand against his chest.

"Darling, you don't need to lay it on so thick," she chided gently.

"But I'm so happy," he replied. He sniffed. "Something smells delicious."

"That's dinner and it's ready, which means you're right on time," Jacinta said. "Come. Abuela is in the kitchen, but she'll want to greet you."

As they entered the dining room, her grandmother appeared carrying a large casserole dish. "Micah. I can call you that now that we're family. Sit everyone. Food should be eaten hot."

Sofia's husband was conspicuously absent, so second cousin Roberto took his seat so Micah could sit by Jacinta. She had to admit, having Micah at Sunday dinner diffused some of the earlier tension.

Sofia said little during dinner, which Jacinta attributed to the fact her cousin wasn't pleased with having her plans thwarted. Abuela filled the conversation gaps by asking about wedding dates and plans. Micah suggested that he and Jacinta marry out at the ranch. "My mother will insist and she won't brook any argument. Will you join us when we tell the rest of the family tonight?"

"Thank you, but I'm tired from working," Abuela answered.

"Perhaps the families can meet later in the week then," Micah said. "My mother will also want to host an engagement party and the rehearsal," he added. "She's been dying to plan those ever since I was little."

It was tradition for the bride's family to pay for the wedding and reception, but there was no way Jacinta's family could afford an event worthy of the Fortune family. She was grateful Micah had skillfully suggested the ceremony and engagement party be held at the ranch. Just one more reason he was so good at being the CEO, good at everything.

"I could make special chocolates for that," Abuela said. "And for the reception, of course."

"That would be so generous of you," Micah said. "Jacinta?"

Tears formed in Jacinta's eyes. "I'd love that," she told her grandmother. "And for you to walk me down the aisle."

Abuela nodded and wiped away her own tears. "Of course. I would be honored."

"I could do everyone's hair," Sofia offered, offering the first smile Jacinta had seen since she'd announced Dan wouldn't be joining them.

"That would also be welcome," Micah said. "Jacinta and I haven't discussed our wedding party yet, but you should, of course, be involved in some capacity. Family matters to both of us."

"It does. I'd love it if you were bridesmaid," Jacinta told her. That olive branch made Sofia's smile widen and, naturally, she accepted. "Rob, you should be a groomsman."

With that settled, Micah lifted Jacinta's hand again. "I hate stealing away my bride-to-be, but my family's waiting. Thank you so much for feeding me. The food was delicious and the company even better."

"I can help clear," Jacinta said, but Abuela rejected the offer with a, "Go, go."

Abuela walked Micah and Jacinta to the front door. "You've made me so happy," she told Jacinta during the hug. She whispered, "He's a good man." She gave her granddaughter a kiss on the cheek. "Now go."

"You've charmed her completely," Jacinta said as she slid into Micah's car. "I hate deluding her."

"I know, which is why you told your friends and I ended up telling my sister and brother today after the undercover interview. Vivienne and Drake will keep our secret. But we do need to remember that, for everyone else, this is a real marriage. Same for us, just without the sex."

Which she was starting to want. Whenever Micah touched her, she lit up like a firecracker. What would it be like to make love to him? "I'm sorry I told my family before you arrived. Sofia got to me and I simply couldn't stand it."

"From here on out, you don't need to. She doesn't even need to be in our wedding party."

Jacinta sighed. "Yeah, she does. She's family. And since we're now having an actual ceremony, I want my three best friends. With Sofia, that's four. Perhaps I shouldn't have added Rob."

"Rob's fine. He's family. I'll ask Rafe, Drake and Shane. Does that work?"

"What about your sister? I don't know her, but she should be in the wedding party, too."

"She'll be thrilled. So, you'll five attendants and to make it even, I'll have my best friend stand in as well. That works. We want this believable, and you deserve a grand wedding." He parked in the circle drive of the family manse. "Ready to face everyone?"

Once outside the car, Jacinta gazed at the overpowering Texas-sized stone mansion. Expressive cars ringed the driveway, indicating a crowd. She touched the butterfly pendant she always wore. Then glanced quickly at the ring on her finger. This was about to become her life, her family. At least for a year. "I'm as ready as I'll ever be."

Micah's grin lasted until he kissed the back of her hand, creating tingles that went to her toes. "Into the fray we go."

Chapter Nine

By the end of the evening, Micah loved how Jacinta fit right in with his extended family. With infinite patience, she'd endured constant oohing and aahing over the ring. She'd won over his mother, who'd welcomed her with open arms. Micah's father had even smiled, a break from his traditional reserve. They'd made him happy by deciding to marry on the ranch.

Once Vivienne had learned they wanted her in the wedding party, Micah's sister had taken charge. "I'm so glad," she gushed as she spoke with Jacinta. "Can you believe my brother suggested a simple courthouse ceremony the other day? *As if.* There was no way I was letting that happen. I'm glad he listened."

"We don't want a huge fuss. The wedding is in a few weeks," Jacinta said.

Vivienne galloped over Jacinta's reservations. "Luckily for you, even though I'm super busy given the thefts, a wedding is right up my alley and it'll make the perfect pick-me-up and be the diversion I need. I'll plan the whole thing."

"But we—" Micah started, only to be cut off as Vivienne kept talking. When he'd suggested to Abuela the wedding be at the ranch, he hadn't necessarily meant something fancy.

"You owe Jacinta more than something simple," Vivienne insisted. "I'll hire the best wedding planner in Emerald Ridge and pass everything by you both so that all you have to do is say yes and no."

As if daring Micah to contradict, Vivienne linked arms with Jacinta. "I've always wanted a sister. Let me do this for you…"

Jacinta glanced at Micah first, but when he shrugged, a smile burst across her face. "Of course. Why not?"

Vivienne squealed her delight. "You and I will have so much fun! This family needs something joyful to keep our minds off certain things." Vivienne let go of Jacinta's arm and nudged her toward Micah. "Brother dear, it's time you kiss your fiancée again."

Micah loosened gritted teeth. While he didn't mind giving Jacinta the wedding of her dreams, he'd told Vivienne the marriage was nothing but a business deal. His younger sister was determined he fall in love. Despite his resolve not to do that, he didn't mind kissing Jacinta. As those around raised their champagne flutes, he gathered her into his arms, lowered his lips to hers and drank from the sweetest nectar known to man. When he reluctantly broke the kiss, Jacinta dipped her head, but not before he saw the desire the kiss had unleashed. She'd been as affected as he. He drew her next to him, where she fit like a missing puzzle piece until his mother stole her away to introduce her to more people. As the news spread, more guests arrived and the family party grew to include some of his parents' best friends who'd dropped by.

"She's fine." Vivienne followed Micah's gaze. "Stop worrying she'll be overwhelmed. Jacinta's doing great. She's a natural at being a member of our family."

"Vivienne," he warned as their brother approached.

She laughed at Micah's discomfort. "Say no more. I

know you have no intentions of this becoming an emotional attachment, but you know what they say about best-laid plans. This marriage might turn real, big brother. It's clear you can't keep your eyes off her. You just won't admit you might have feelings."

"You know what I told you," Micah hedged as his sister hit close to the bull's-eye of what he feared most—an emotional entanglement. "Nothing will happen between us. Besides, I'm not sure I'm ready to open up again."

Vivienne placed a comforting hand on his shoulder. "Micah, I know how much your ex hurt you. But not every woman is like her. I can already see Jacinta is not like that. She's as far opposite as one can get. Do not compare them."

Micah's jaw tightened. "It's not a comparison. It's going into this marriage with my eyes open and my heart closed. Yes, my ex cheated on me and then had the audacity to claim she was pregnant with my child, only to disappear when I found out the truth about both the cheating and her lies about there even being a baby. This is not a case of 'once you fall off the horse you get back on.' It's about the fact Jacinta and I have a business arrangement."

"I understand your fear. But you can't let one bad experience close you off from love forever. I see the way Jacinta looks at you, the way you two are together. The way you refuse to feel because it's easier not to trust anyone holds you down. Don't let your past rob you of true happiness."

Drake clapped Micah on the shoulder. "I agree with Vivienne. What she said."

"How's the Gift of Fortune nominations going?" Micah asked, ready to get his siblings to focus on something else besides his relationship. In a surprise twist, Rafe had met the love of his life, struggling single mother Heidi Markham, who'd been one of the recipients in need of an emotionally healing week's stay at the Fortune's Gold Ranch and Spa. Now they were engaged to be married and planning a wedding of their own. Those who were chosen for the initiative found everything at the ranch free of charge and available with a call to the concierge. "I haven't looked at many nominations lately, not after doing that one set," he added, turning to Vivienne. "Which ones did you like?"

"They are so hard to choose. It's so difficult," she said. "There's this one young mother whose husband died, leaving her with triplets. Her mother sent in the nomination. Then there's the one from one of Emerald Ridge's principals about a teacher in his building who was recently diagnosed with breast cancer. Another one's from a group of volunteers who want to honor someone they affectionately call the cat lady. She runs the local animal shelter and is into trapping, neutering and returning feral cats to help reduce the cat overpopulation. You know all of our barn cats are TNR'd."

"Those are some worthy candidates," Micah agreed.

Vivienne nodded. "I know. I wish I could invite all of the nominees. I can't believe Drake is making me choose."

Drake shrugged. "It's how it works. Take it up with Rafe."

Vivienne faked a pout. "It's half you, too! I want them all to have a special week at the ranch. The program is such a great thing."

Talk then turned to ranch business, and afterward, Micah retrieved Jacinta to return her home.

"That went well," she told him as they drove.

"It did. My family adores you." *I adore you.* That fact unsettled him. When he let her go, his family would be disappointed. He would miss her. It was one reason he'd kept himself emotionally closed off from anyone but family. Besides being lusted after for his last name and actual monetary fortune, being blind to his last girlfriend's disregard of their relationship had made him gun-shy. Thankfully, he hadn't actually asked his ex to marry him, just thought about it and bought the ring.

As for Jacinta, Micah knew she wasn't like that, but then again, she'd agreed to marry him because he'd offered her a way to meet her grandmother's ultimatum. Although, admittedly, the nuptials had been *his* idea. But he'd had no choice. She'd been ready to give up on her dreams. Maybe it was like the Gift of Fortune program. He was simply hardwired to help. Either that or there was more going on that he didn't want to think about.

"How'd the interview go with your siblings?" Jacinta asked.

"Rather amusing. No clue how they didn't laugh through it. Since I obviously got the job, I'll be in the office tomorrow morning, and then out on the ranch starting on Tuesday. I'll be gone for several days. I shouldn't have moved you into your position yet. You were always so capable of managing things when I'm gone."

"I'll make sure my replacement can do the same. Your cover story is that you're in Dallas, right?"

"You're the best." He meant it, and since they were on a safe straightway, he moved his hand to briefly cover hers. His fingers missed her touch when he returned them to the wheel. "And yeah, if anyone asks, I'm in Dallas. I'll call or text you every night to see how things are. Besides, that way the guys on the ranch will believe I have a gal back home, which I do."

"I hope you catch the person who's doing all this."

"Me, too." He glanced over as a truck pulling a trailer passed them going the opposite direction. As he'd been doing since the thefts, he glanced at the horses inside. None appeared to be theirs. "The start of this year has been so stressful for my family. Like Vivienne said, a wedding will be a good pick-me-up."

"I hope so. Poppy let me hold Joey and he's the sweetest baby. I can't believe the mother would demand half a million for him. If she even *is* the mother. If I had a child, no one would ever take him from me."

The darkness of the car's interior hid her expression, but Micah heard some wistfulness in her tone. "You want children?" They hadn't discussed kids because they weren't planning on a physical relationship.

"Someday. Maybe after I'm twenty-eight or something? I have a business to build. My grandmother may think that having kids young is great, like she, my dad and Sofia did, but I'd rather be older and more established. There's also artificial insemination if I don't find a partner. One of my college professors did that and she's very happy."

He couldn't imagine Jacinta at a sperm bank. He stopped himself before he volunteered to help her the natural way. "You'll find the right man and have everything you want, including marriage and family. Part of me wants to apologize for taking a year out of your life."

His words came out sincere, but Micah realized he didn't mean them wholeheartedly. He liked having her in his life. Perhaps he was a fool for even thinking of letting her go. And their chemistry? He gripped the wheel tighter. "Sometimes I wonder why I suggested it. I just want you to be happy."

"I'm the one who said yes. I'm getting my grandmother's company in return, so it's all good," Jacinta reassured him. "I'm grateful for that. I'll have everything else on my timetable."

His brain made a leap to picturing Jacinta pregnant with

his child, and he concentrated on staying to the right of the double yellow lines. He couldn't go down that rabbit hole. He was much older and far too jaded to be the right man for her. "I'm certain you will get exactly what you want when you want it."

"I appreciate your confidence."

Micah noticed that Abuela had left the porch light on as he put the car in Park. "I'll see you in the morning." The curtains flickered. "We have an audience."

"You're lucky that I like your kisses," she teased.

"I like yours, too." He'd never been more honest. Micah leaned to cover her mouth with his. He'd planned a brief kiss, but the moment their lips touched, he found himself lost. Desire flooded through him, reminding him that while he may have shut off his emotions, his libido was alive and well. He craved her. More than he cared to admit. He wrapped his hand around the back of her neck and brought her closer. Deepening the kiss, he forgot where he was until the porch light flickered on and off several times.

Still dazed by the sensations, he drew back and leaned his forehead to hers. "You meant it when you said your grandmother was old-fashioned, didn't you?" he whispered as the light flashed again.

"Sadly yes." She moved back, the porch light illuminating her big brown eyes. The kiss had obviously affected her as well. "Another benefit to being married to you will be that I'll be more independent."

"Move in with me now." The moment the impulsive words left his mouth, he realized he meant them. He slid his house key off his fob and wrapped her fingers around it. "*Mi casa es su casa.* Don't wait until the wedding."

"I'll think about it. Perhaps the Monday after Mother's

Day. That's a week. I don't want to be in that empty house without you. At least not while you're undercover."

"Fair," Micah agreed. "But no later than next Monday. That'll give you a week to pack. I'll walk you to the door."

He exited the driver's side, assisted her from the passenger side, and then held her hand as they walked to the front porch. Abuela opened the screen door before he could reach for the handle. "Good night," he told Jacinta before dropping one last light kiss on her lips.

He waited while she stepped inside. Then turned away once the door closed and the porch light extinguished. As he reached the car, his phone buzzed with a text from Jacinta. I had a great time tonight. She'd added one red heart, which he refused to read too much into.

He sent her back a smiley face along with Me too.

As his phone buzzed again, his excitement jumped. What had she responded?

But the text was from Vivienne, telling him they'd had another attempt at a theft. She'd written We scared the person away, but it was close. We almost lost another horse.

Micah bit back the curses that threatened as he rushed toward the ranch. They had to put a stop to this. He couldn't get undercover soon enough.

When Jacinta stepped inside the house, she found Abuela's arms folded across her chest. "What?" she asked.

"You should not be making out in a car," her grandmother scolded.

Jacinta managed to avoid rolling her eyes. She was twenty-six, not sixteen. "I was kissing him goodbye. He's my fiancé."

The word, which had seemed so impossible to say days ago, rolled off her tongue with ease.

"As long as you are marrying him for the right reasons," Abuela said. "You will get my company and not Sofia. But is he what you want? *Who* you want?"

Jacinta found herself surprised by the questions. "Did you not see me kissing him? If that's not proof, I don't know what is." Her passion in the car had not been faked. Whenever Micah touched her, her body combusted. "He makes me happy." That was also true. "We're very much in sync." Again a truth.

"And he loves you?" Abuela's gaze probed Jacinta's face as if looking for any shred of doubt. "This isn't some hero worship on your part? Micah Fortune is a powerful man. He's older. He can provide you a lifestyle beyond your wildest dreams."

Also true, but that was not why she was marrying him. Jacinta firmed her resolve. She wouldn't be in this situation if Abuela hadn't made her ultimatum. "He's not that much older. We work well together." She reminded herself to keep sticking with the facts. So far, she was doing fine.

"And you love him."

"Of course." Jacinta said the words with a straight face. Her declaration wasn't actually a lie. If nothing else, she loved him as a friend. She'd loved working for him. As for falling in love, it would be too easy. She had to shut off her emotions the same way he had, for loving him would complicate matters. In a year, when she walked away after they called it quits, she needed to do so with her head high and heart intact.

Abuela loosened her arms. "Then I'm satisfied. I only want your happiness, you know that."

"I do and I love you for it." Jacinta gave her grandmother a hug. "I'm going to hate moving out next week, but at least Uncle Luis is here to keep you company."

"Next week!" Abuela stepped away. "You're moving out? Already?"

"Yes. I see no reason to wait. And, most likely on Mother's Day, we'll need to go to the Fortunes' so you can meet everyone. Vivienne told me they always have a joint event to celebrate her mom and her aunt. We've got so many events upcoming, like graduation the Saturday after that and then the wedding the following weekend."

"It's moving so fast." Abuela touched the small gold cross at her neck. A gift from Jacinta's father, she never took it off.

Despite her grandmother's sudden reservations, Jacinta wasn't going to let her grandmother off the hook. "You're the one who established the deadline for me to marry. Micah and I don't want to rush, but you gave us no choice if I'm to follow all my dreams."

Abuela used the back of her hand to wipe a tear away. "Maybe I was too hasty. Now that it's happening, I'm going to miss you."

That softened Jacinta's heart and she gave her grandmother a huge hug. "I'll be twenty minutes away at most, so we'll see each other often. I'll always be a Gomez despite becoming a Fortune."

"As long as you give me grandbabies. Sofia's are too big now for me to cuddle."

"I'll see what I can do," Jacinta said, making a promise she intended to keep someday, but not anywhere in the near future, and not with Micah. "It's late. We both should go to bed. You've got to ship chocolates tomorrow and I'm at the office bright and early. In the afternoon, Micah's leaving for a conference, and I've got to train my replacement. Plus, I start working with my new colleagues in my new role."

Abuela gave a bittersweet but happy smile, the kind

where you know your dreams for your family are coming true but also meant everything changes. "Your parents would be so proud of you. *Te amo, mi querida nieta.* You make me so proud."

Jacinta bit back the tears at her grandmother's outpouring of love. "*Te amo mi querida abuela.* You're the best grandmother a girl could have. Now, let's go to bed."

Jacinta crawled under her covers later that night and drew the light duvet to her chin. Marrying Micah was doing the right thing for everyone. Her engagement had made Abuela so happy. But part of Jacinta couldn't let go that this marriage was a business deal. A charade.

Unless they fell in love. *And pigs could fly, too.* That's how probable it was that Micah would grow to love her. Frustrated and restless, Jacinta tossed and turned and banged her fist into the pillow to make it more comfortable. She lay on her back and stared up at a ceiling still covered with the glow-in-the-dark stars she'd added when she'd been ten. They glimmered faintly, their magical powers having faded over the last sixteen years. She'd always known her time in this room would come to an end. Life moved on, and she had a man to marry and a company to build. She closed her eyes and Micah's handsome image swam in her imagination. A sigh shuddered through her. She was getting everything she wanted. The company. Micah for a year. An opportunity to reach her goals. Just as long as she remembered love was not part of the deal.

Chapter Ten

By noon Monday, Micah decided that everything was more or less back to normal. Members of his office staff had appeared shocked by the announcement of his and Jacinta's engagement, but they'd quickly expressed their congratulations and seemed genuinely happy. Micah's new administrative assistant settled in, and Micah expected Jacinta would have the man running at full speed before Micah returned Friday after his stint undercover. The Fortunes were hosting a charity gala at the Emerald Ridge Hotel Saturday night, which would be when he and Jacinta would make their official public debut as an engaged couple. Micah anticipated a drama-free gathering, but he knew that he and Jacinta wouldn't escape the curious stares as everyone scrutinized his new fiancée.

A knock sounded and Jacinta entered. He took in her appearance, liking how today her braided hair fell in a long, thick tail down her back. Micah loved her hair loose, but when she wore it off her face, her features seemed even more expressive and her light brown eyes more luminous. When she lifted one of those perfectly arched brows, he realized he was staring. "Hey," he greeted, remaining seated as part of him had risen to attention.

"You weren't answering your cell phone," she chided

gently. "Vivienne called me and wanted me to tell you that you have to check your texts."

"How enterprising of her." His sister was already roping Jacinta into the wife role of finding the missing husband. But Micah had been busy. He reached into his pocket and swiped open his family's text message thread.

"Is everything okay?" Eyebrows he wanted to trace with his finger knit together in concern.

He set the phone on the desk. "The DNA tests have been delayed. Poppy went by the lab and demanded to know why. They said we should know more by next week. I don't even want to think that Jennifer Johnson could be Joey's mother. She's a horrible person."

Jacinta moved closer to his desk. "Nothing you can do until the results come back."

"Yeah, I need to focus on finding the saboteur." More composed, he rose. They moved to sit on his office sofa. "It'll be different, not seeing you until the gala. Unless I catch this guy sooner…"

"I'll be busy, too. Besides work, your sister has me coming and going. She told me I couldn't wear the same dress from the dinner with Alan, which is ridiculous, so we're going shopping Thursday afternoon. Then I'm her and Poppy's guest at the spa all day Saturday, getting buffed and scrubbed."

"I'm not sure if that sounds lovely or painful," Micah said. Jacinta sat primly, with her hands in her lap. He reached for one of her hands and toyed with her fingers, delighted to see she didn't pull away. "I'm glad that you and my sister are becoming friends."

"I think we will be good friends. She's a dynamo, and I can respect that. I thought I was an overachiever, but your sister already has my wedding dress appointment set at

Emerald Ridge Weddings. The planner just started two hours ago."

Emerald Ridge Weddings was an exclusive bridal boutique, so he knew Jacinta would be in good hands and get only the best. "When Vivienne sets her mind to something, she's a steamroller. Don't let her push you around or choose anything you don't want."

Her forehead wrinkled and he resisted the urge to smooth it.

"It's already overwhelming. I don't necessarily need a fancy wedding. We can keep things lower key. It's not real. Why are we pretending it is and spending all this money?"

"Because it *is* real," Micah reminded her. He lifted her hand to his lips and kissed the back. "You're becoming the wife of a CEO. You're marrying a Fortune."

"I still like the idea of eloping to Vegas." She attempted a half smile.

"But I don't." He didn't, he realized. "You deserve the best and I plan on giving it you. It makes me happy when I can give you things."

"If I'm honest, it makes me uncomfortable."

That was one reason why she was so perfect and why he was willing to marry her. Jacinta might be getting her grandmother's company and his money, but she wasn't an opportunist. "Can you try to tolerate the wedding for my sake? Let me spoil you, not because you're earning it, but because I like doing it. I'm enjoying myself and you deserve some pampering."

"I can try," she said with a sigh. "But I doubt I'll ever get used to it."

He laced his fingers through hers. "Good. I hope you don't. That's another reason we're so perfect for each other. You keep me grounded. You're not afraid to tell me when

I'm being foolish. But, as for the wedding, we're not making your grandmother sit through a town hall ceremony. That, I can't abide. Besides, think of it this way. We're putting money into the local economy."

"I know you're right, but that still doesn't mean I have to like it. I don't want to be a kept woman living off her husband's wealth. You're already giving me a ridiculous allowance."

"I will never see you as such." He meant it, so he changed the subject. "Your last meeting with your adviser is this week, right?"

"Yes. While you're gone. A final gathering for those in my MBA cohort. My degree is done. Just need the parchment."

"I'm arranging a celebratory dinner for after your graduation. Do you have a preference where you'd like to go? I was thinking the private room at Lone Star Selects."

"Really, it's not…" she began.

He put a finger to her soft and supple lips. "It is necessary. An MBA is worthy achievement needing to be celebrated. Let me. Please." When she nodded, his finger fell away with a pop and slid to cup her chin. "Good. Now, I think we should practice kissing a bit more, don't you?" Not that they had any reason to, but Micah wanted to feel her lips beneath his. "Do you want to kiss me?"

"I do."

"That's it. Practice saying those words." He liked the sound of them. He brought his mouth to hers, gently at first until the same inferno that had consumed him last night began. Unable to help himself, he let the passionate current take him away. He kissed her with raw need and hunger, and then, unable to take it any longer, he slid his mouth to her neck, kissing her silky skin. Jacinta whimpered her desire and, like a man possessed, Micah slid his hand lower, finding her breast. She shifted to give him access and he slid his fingers beneath the silk V of her shirt. His thumb flicked her nipple before his mouth found it, and then she leaned against the back of the couch so he could devour her like a man starved for food. His free hand slid under her skirt, finding her wet and ready. He shifted her panties and slid a finger in, and Jacinta quaked around him. He brought his mouth back to hers, adding more fingers until she closed her eyes, gripped his arm and shook as she came. He'd never seen anything so beautiful.

As her orgasm subsided, she opened her eyes and he kissed her softly on the lips. He'd risked something today, pushing the boundaries and changing the rules he'd set for their relationship. "Don't say that was a mistake." He could hear the plea in his voice. Don't let her reject him. He couldn't bear it.

"No. I..." She found her breath and a satisfied smile crept over her flushed face. "That was good. Not in our plan, but we're marrying. Maybe the plan can change."

"I'd like that. I'm finding it difficult to keep my hands off you. If I didn't have to leave..." Bad enough he'd not even locked his office door. Thankfully he'd kept his wits. He wanted their first time to be proper, in a bed, not some fast coupling on his office couch. He put his fingers into his mouth—a mistake—for one taste was not enough. He wanted to spread her and bring her to another climax using nothing but his tongue. Instead, he set her clothes to right and slid his hand behind her neck. He touched his forehead to hers. "I can't fight the attraction I have for you. You're driving me crazy, even more so because you're wearing my ring."

She slid her thumbs against his lips. "I want you, too. But you have to go or you'll arrive late. We have all the time we need. We can continue this later, right?"

"Right." Micah helped Jacinta to her feet. He kissed her once more and then set her aside with an anguished groan. If he didn't get to the door, he'd never leave for the ranch. He grabbed his phone and made for the doorway, turning back to look at the woman he'd just ravaged. For the first time in his life, the right words failed. He had so much to tell her, but nothing would come. "Take care and I'll call you tonight."

Jacinta watched as Micah strode through the door and closed it behind him. She then power walked into his bathroom, locked the door and worked on getting herself together. Moments ago, she'd let Micah bring her to orgasm. She placed her palms on both sides of her face and blew out a deep breath. Not just any orgasm, either. The best she'd ever experienced.

And she wanted more. If he hadn't broken things off because he'd had to leave—and she knew his schedule as well as he did—she would have let him continue. She reached for her phone. This situation called for an emergency meeting of her friends. Within two minutes, everyone had confirmed they'd meet at four thirty for happy hour.

Jacinta wasn't certain how she made it through the rest of the day, but as no one gave her curious looks, she somewhat relaxed. She'd met the sales team before as Micah's assistant, and once in her new role, they welcomed her kindly. Her duties used more of her MBA skills, and her new boss put her on a project analyzing the data to predict future performance and trends. Micah's new assistant interrupted her a few times with questions, making the time until happy hour pass even faster.

Her friends were waiting when she arrived. "I'm going to sleep with Micah," she told them almost the moment she slid onto her barstool.

"Well, of course you are," Kim said with a huge grin. "That's a given."

"We saw that coming from a mile away," Carolyn added with a "sorry not sorry" expression. "The man is irresistibly handsome."

"At least you didn't bury the lead," Katie finished, pouring red wine into Jacinta's glass. She set the empty bottle to the side.

"My marriage is supposed to be in name only." Jacinta took a long sip. Her friends had ordered her favorite Pinot Noir. "But every time we kiss, I don't want to stop."

"How could you? That man is gorgeous," Katie said. "I'd kiss him if he were my fiancé."

"Yeah, it's natural to want him," Kim added. "You two are in control. You can change the rules to anything you want."

Jacinta thrust the ring forward. "Look at this. I googled how much this stone cost. It's pricier than a diamond. He's determined to give me the wedding of my dreams. Who does that when it's not a love match?"

"Oh. You're afraid you'll fall for him," Carolyn said sagely. "You're the one afraid of falling in love."

"I might be falling already," Jacinta admitted, draining the wine as if it were life force. When their server arrived with appetizers, Kim told him to bring another bottle. "He's sworn off love."

Katie scoffed. "Men always say that. It's a plotline in every book or movie."

"Micah's different. He never says or does anything he doesn't mean. He's been that way ever since I've known him. This is a practical marriage. We don't love each other." She reached for her water glass to avoid thinking about how easily it would be to totally fall for the man. "It's just complicated by the fact I want to have sex."

"It's clear he wants to sleep with you, too, whether he loves you or not. There are relationships built on less," Kim said. "I say you enjoy it."

"I'm not sure that's comforting." A sip of cool water brought little relief. "Part of me feels like I'm selling my soul for Abuela's business. The other part of me is excited to be Micah's wife, not only because of the doors that being his wife opens but because I like being around him. He's fun and interesting. Determined. Kind. Generous." She decided not to tell them he was going undercover at the ranch. It was one thing to discuss her business or fake marriage with her friends, especially as he'd only entrusted her with the secret because of their engagement, but telling them about his top-secret plans to bring down the saboteur would be crossing the line. "He's fun. We can talk about anything. We *do* talk about anything," she amended.

"We get that Micah's a good guy and that you like him. You're about to share a house and there's chemistry between you. So if things happen, let them," Kim said. "What can it hurt?"

"She doesn't want to get her heart broken," Carolyn pointed out, ever the practical one.

"Then go into anything physical with your eyes wide open and you won't get hurt. You know the marriage has an expiration date, so enjoy him while it lasts," Katie said. "When do you see him next?"

"He's out of town for week. He said he'd call me each night to chat."

"That's sweet," Carolyn said.

"It's perfect," Kim said. "His trip will give you some time away from him, out of his godlike aura of tractor-beam masculinity. You'll chat on the phone and get to know each other in your new engaged capacity. That should allow for some perspective on each side." She shrugged. "If the heart is, like, 'oh, this was a blip,' you'll know to put some space between you. But if by the end of the week you can't wait to kiss him again because you've become so connected, then jump the man's bones. Whatever you decide, know that we'll support you one hundred percent."

"I appreciate that. You three are the best."

"You better believe it," Kim said. She lifted a chicken wing. "Why isn't anyone eating?"

Their server arrived carrying the second bottle of wine. Jacinta waited until her friends had filled their glasses and plates before talking again.

"Speaking of support, I'll need your help with the wedding prep. The planner texted and told me that as long as we go by the boutique and get your measurements done tomorrow afternoon, anything they have in stock can be altered and made ready. Same for my dress."

"You mean we're going to say yes to dresses tomorrow?" Katie's grin widened.

"Hopefully." Jacinta dipped a tortilla chip into the spinach dip. After draining a glass of wine, she needed food. "The appointment is at four. You'll get to meet Vivienne, Micah's sister. She's in the wedding party, too. Abuela will be there. And Sofia, since she's in the wedding. You know, family."

"No worries." Kim lifted another barbecued chicken wing but stopped before she bit into it. "We'll be there. Even better, we'll keep your cousin in line."

"Nothing is going to get in the way of you getting your dress and your man," Katie vowed. "Nothing. He's going to be all yours."

Jacinta hoped that was true.

Micah had been in the bunkhouse multiple times, but never as a new, temporary employee. Like almost every other house on the property, the bunkhouse was divided into two wings. However, since the wranglers—those who managed the horses for the spa and those who worked with the horse breeding operation—outnumbered the number of men working with the cattle three-to-one, the wings weren't evenly divided. The wranglers provided trail rides and lessons, and they cared for approximately fifty horses. They organized and polished tack, ensured the corral was clean and safe, and moved horses in and out of pastures. Many of the workers had been with the Fortunes for over a decade and were not only experts on assisting guests ride, but they also ensured the Fortunes bred the best horses. Micah hated to think that a long-time employee could be compromised and harming the ranch.

The number of permanent ranch hands needed for managing the cattle was far fewer, and when extra drovers were required, extra workers like Micah were hired. To protect the grazing lands and allow the grasses to regrow, this week the drovers would move the cattle from the northwest quadrant to the northeast. While the job could be done using trucks, drones and ATVs, the Fortunes liked using horsemen known as drovers to herd the cattle from one area to the next. They'd found the cattle didn't stress or spook as easily, lessening the risk of a stampede. As the cattle drives were often an activity that the guests could watch from a safe distance, keeping everyone and the animals safe was paramount.

Since it was considered bad luck to place a cowboy hat on a bed, Micah instead hung his on the hook in the tall locker assigned to him. In cowboy lore and superstition, putting his hat on the bed or placing it brim-side down anywhere meant he was courting bad luck that could bring about an argument, injury or death. As he had a wedding to attend and a thief and saboteur to catch, he needed all the luck he could get.

He put away the rest of his things, donned his hat and headed for the mess hall. When he arrived, dinner was in full swing. As he stepped inside, he noted the wranglers sat together, as did the drovers. He'd guessed correctly that the men would wear their hats in the mess hall. If this were a restaurant, they'd perhaps take them off, but the cafeteria line and eating area set aside for the ranch hands didn't count as being formal enough to warrant removal.

He went through the line and located the men he'd be working with. As the last man hired and arriving at dinner, he sat at the far end of the table. The guy across from him, his mouth full of corn on the cob, grunted and gave him a chin-dip in acknowledgment. The man to Micah's left wiped the fingers of his left hand on a paper napkin and extended it across his chest.

"Raleigh, but you can call me Rowdy," he said.

Micah's elbow bent awkwardly at his side as he shook with the wrong hand. "Toby."

"Yeah, bosses said you'd be coming tonight." Rowdy pointed down at the men who'd interviewed Micah. "Bosses got a bee in their bonnet since the cattle needs movin' but we're supposed to get strong storms that'll bring some flash flooding, so we're polishing leather tomorrow."

Lifting a baby back rib, Micah shrugged. "Pays the same. Rather not get wet."

"Number of times I've been drenched…" Rowdy laughed before realizing he was talking with his mouth full. "Doin' this job and movin' on."

"Where you from?" Micah asked.

"Up by Amarillo, near Canyon. Move around a lot. Usually spend summers in Montana. Used to do a little rodeo but hurt my back and had to quit. But still can sit the saddle well enough to make me some good money. Fortunes pay really well, so I keep comin' back."

Micah chewed some corn, his silence a green light for Rowdy to keep talking.

"Yeah, got me a little spread I've been eyein'. Maybe by the end of the summer, if the widow don't sell it by then. I let her know, but you know how that goes. Families want to put their fingers and input into everything." Rowdy shook his head.

"Yeah, I get that. Hope you can manage to get it." Micah wasn't sure what else to say. The men surrounding them didn't even appear to be listening to the conversation. They'd apparently realized Rowdy liked to talk and had tuned him out. As the new guy, Micah was stuck.

"What about you? What's your deal?" Rowdy asked.

"Ah, same as you. Been around a bit. Trying to get ahead. Want to marry my girl." Micah and his siblings had come up with the perfect backstory.

"Yeah, I got me an old lady," Rowdy said. "No kids, though."

"Me either." Micah's involuntary shudder was seen by those around him.

"What's wrong with kids? Got me three." The guy across the table's curiosity had gotten the best of him and he'd joined the conversation. "'Course it's hard to get the time to see them."

"Only because they're in Tucson and you hate to fly," the man to Rowdy's left said. He leaned over Rowdy to look at Micah. "I'm Chance. Good to have you. Don't let Rowdy get on your nerves."

"You're the one who gets on everyone's nerves," someone else countered, and then as Micah worried that the men were getting riled, he realized it was good-natured teasing, the kind of grief men give each other after a long day of hard labor.

"So your gal, she pretty? Mine is." Rowdy showed Micah his lock screen, which contained the image of Rowdy with his arm around a big-haired blonde.

"Nice." In Micah's opinion, Jacinta was far prettier. "Mine's gorgeous. But she hates photos so she won't give me one." The reality was he had plenty of pictures of her from the family dinner, but as Micah, not Toby.

Rowdy scoffed. "I don't even think you got a gal. Get 'r to send you a selfie so I believe it."

To save face, Micah said, "I'll ask her when I call her tonight."

"Yeah, you better. Not much signal when we get deep out into the ranch."

The cook had set out dessert and the men bussed their dinner plates and exchanged them for slices of carrot cake. After eating, the workers returned to the bunkhouse. Making sure his laptop couldn't be observed, Micah sat on his bed and logged onto the private Fortune Wi-Fi network. He had nothing in his email that required immediate attention, so he logged off. A bunch of guys played darts in the common room and others played foosball. A few watched TV and the loners played handheld games on either portable devices or their phones. With a glance at his screen, Micah noted the time and went back to his bunk to video call Jacinta.

When Jacinta saw Micah's number come across her phone, she was feeling the residual effects of drinking two glasses of wine and eating heavy carbs. She wasn't drunk by any means, but the wine had mellowed her enough to make her sleepy and she'd crawled into bed early. The moment the phone rang, she was wide awake.

"Hey. How'd today go?" she asked as Micah's disguised face came into view. If she didn't know his number and his voice, she'd have sworn a stranger had the wrong number.

He leaned closer and filled the screen. "As well as expected. How about you?"

"Went to an impromptu happy hour with my friends, drank two glasses of wine, ate appetizers and told my besties they better be on time tomorrow to help me pick a dress." She left out that she'd told them about what had happened in the office and that she wanted to sleep with him.

Micah's deep rich voice chuckled. "You sound a bit overwhelmed by the wedding prep."

"A little," she admitted. "But my friends know about our arrangement, as does your sister, so I'll have good backup while I'm shopping tomorrow."

"As long as you find a good dress. No, scratch that. I *want* you to find a great dress. One that knocks my socks off."

She nibbled her lower lip as his words washed over her. "Really?"

The camera tilted sideways to show the ceiling but his voice came through loud and clear. "Really. When you come down that aisle, I want you to wow me. I want to be bowled over. Then, trust me, at the end of the night, rest assured I'm taking it off you. So find a great dress. You can do that, can't you?"

"I can try." To hide her body's reaction to his words, she pulled the covers to her chin as Micah's face came back into focus. When he'd called, she'd been reading a cozy mystery.

"Do more than try. Do it for me. I'd tell you to lower that comforter, but I'm in the bunkhouse. But I'm thinking about you and can't wait until our wedding night. We're going to write our own rules."

"I'm thinking about that, too." The words came out far huskier than she wanted. Did he know how affected she was? She wished she could see his true face to know if he meant what he said or if he was just acting for the men who surely had to be nearby. "Do you like your coworkers?"

He noted the change of subject. "So far. Rowdy doesn't believe you're real."

"I never said that!" Jacinta heard a distant male voice shout out.

That made her pause. Maybe Micah's words about a wedding night had been an act. She powered through her disappointment. "Well, you tell Rowdy…in fact, turn the camera around and I'll do it."

Micah complied. "She wants to talk to you," he called.

"Hello?" The male voice was louder and a man around Jacinta's age crowded into view next to Micah.

"You must be Rowdy," she greeted him. "Don't give my man any grief."

"You sure you're not his sister covering for him?"

Tucked in bed, Jacinta was glad all Rowdy could see was her face. "He doesn't have a sister. Now, go away so I can talk to him."

"Yes, ma'am." Laughing, she heard Rowdy move off.

"He's gone," Micah said, entirely on screen again.

"Seems nice. Glad you're making friends."

Micah nodded. "Not sure about the friends part, but at least fitting in."

"Well, call me tomorrow. I'm a bit tired and wanted to turn in early and read. Take care and I'll talk to you tomorrow. I'll let you know if I found a dress."

"Sounds good, beautiful. Sleep well."

"I'll try," she promised. She certainly didn't need another restless night where he haunted her dreams.

"Sweet dreams. Miss you. Good night." Before she could answer, he'd disconnected. Jacinta placed her cell phone on the bedside table. He'd missed her? Her heart gave a jump before she calmed herself. His words were most likely for Rowdy's benefit. She had to remember that his feelings weren't real. Even if she wished they were.

Micah snuck out of the bunkhouse after everyone fell asleep. When he met Vivienne and Drake outside the stables, Drake handed him a shotgun.

"I'll get some rest and take over for you at two a.m." Drake glanced at Micah. "You sure you can go tomorrow on four hours of sleep? Breakfast is at six and you got a long day ahead of you."

"Yeah, I'm sure," Micah said. "This shift's mine."

"I'm patrolling with you," Vivienne told him as Drake left. "Shane's taking over for me when Drake returns."

Micah let his eyes adjust to the darkness. A light breeze whispered through the grass. Insects chirped. An occasional pawing of horse hooves and soft whinnies could be heard coming from the barn. The moonless sky was clear, which made it hard to believe that heavy rain would start around the same time his alarm sounded. "Should we make the rounds?" he asked.

"Yeah. I was thinking we could split up," Vivienne suggested.

Even if she was armed, Micah didn't like the idea of his sister encountering a thief. "Let's stay together. Walk me around the ranch. It's been a while since I've been out here at night."

The two of them entered the barn to ensure the horses

were secure. Satisfied they were safely bedded down, Vivienne reset the alarm. Far off, they could see a pair of headlights moving in the distance. "That's the security staff manning the perimeter," she told him. "My biggest worries are that someone can sneak onto the property through the guest ranch or that our person is working for us."

"Are the additional cameras operational?" Micah had seen new ones being installed.

"Yes. We added some after Shane's horse was taken. Even more before the latest attempt." They walked to the outdoor corral and noticed nothing seemed amiss. Micah glanced at the heavens, locating the various planets and constellations dotting the deep night sky.

"Jacinta told me wedding gown shopping is tomorrow." He kept his voice low.

"It is. The planner is positive if she finds something, it will be ready. Same for the bridesmaids' dresses. Did Jacinta tell you we also need to go to the boutique and find dresses for the engagement party and the charity event? I insisted."

"Be careful not to scare her. She's not happy about the trappings of my wealth or the fact she has to keep shopping."

Moving in the shadows as they were, he sensed rather than saw Vivienne's smile. "Good. That means you've found a keeper. Unlike… I'm not even going to say her name. How dare she tell you she was pregnant and be cheating on you?"

"Yeah, yeah. I was a blind fool. I'm not making that mistake again." Although the pain he had once felt didn't create the same derision. Somehow his anger had softened after he'd put a ring on Jacinta's finger. "Now that I have Jacinta, my heart is protected."

His sister snorted. "Sorry. Bug flew in my nose." Micah didn't believe that for a minute.

"I'm serious," he said. "We have legal paperwork and everything to outline our relationship. It's spelled out."

Vivienne sighed. "I'm going to play devil's advocate. When you swore off emotional entanglements, that was because you'd been with the wrong woman. Perhaps Jacinta's the exact *right* woman. What if she's the one you've been waiting for? You seem happier and more content when she's around. Grounded even. You're marrying her, so maybe you need to open your heart and let her in. Why don't you try? What would it hurt?"

Micah dodged the question. "What about you, sis? You date, sure, but nothing ever gets serious. Horses and cattle get more attention."

Vivienne lifted her arm and Micah assumed she was brushing her hair back as she so often did. "I like horses and cattle far better. Besides, fate will drop the right guy into my life. He'll find me."

It was Micah's turn to snort. "If you say so."

"That's my story and I'm sticking to it," she insisted. "That's how it will happen."

Micah turned serious. "I do hope you find someone. I want you happy. It's hard, isn't it, with our cousins trotting around with their partners like they're show ponies? We've become the old nags in the stable, failing in our purpose. There is nothing wrong with being single."

"Our cousins' engagements do add a layer of parental pressure that wasn't there before," Vivienne agreed. "At the same time, those same engagements put things into perspective. I do want more. I don't want to be alone my entire life. And you shouldn't either." She sighed. "You're a great guy, Micah, and you deserve to be happy. You lead the way in everything else, so maybe do the same with this and show me and Drake how it's done. Take off your jaded, woe-is-me glasses and take a hard look at Jacinta. What if she's the one?"

"If she is, it'll be a good thing I'm already married to her." Micah made light of his sister's assertion because thinking too deeply about Jacinta being the one would make him examine set-in-stone life tenets best left alone. He'd had one heartbreak and didn't want another. Already he and Jacinta had upped the stakes sexually, and he desired her more than anyone he'd ever met. "Shall we skirt around the bunkhouse and check the employee parking lot?"

With that, conversation about their personal lives ceased. By the time 2:00 a.m. rolled around, Micah was tired. When Shane and Drake relieved him and Vivienne, Micah was beyond ready for some shut-eye. "Get some rest," Drake teased. "You'll be polishing away tomorrow."

"So I heard."

Micah crept back into the bunkhouse and fell asleep the moment his head hit the pillow. The next morning, when he headed into the mess hall, the entire place was filled with loud conversations. "What's going on?" he asked as he sat down.

Rowdy lifted a piece of sausage link. "A rustler struck at the Wellington Ranch! Got away with two horses. Loaded 'em up and hauled 'em away."

"Wow." Micah cut into his waffle. "That's bad."

"Yeah. Things been happening in these parts for a while. Be on extra lookout." Rowdy leaned closer. "No one's been able to catch the guy."

Micah didn't tell Rowdy that he planned on doing just that. Instead, he let the conversation go on without him, listening intently as the men around him speculated on who could have done it, where the horses might be sold and which ranch might be hit next. He hoped he'd hear anything new, but instead the chatter was a rehash of everything he already knew. Then their boss stood, gave the men their assignments, and as thunder clapped outside, Micah readied for a day of cleaning saddles and tack.

"You must be the bride!" the wedding planner said the moment Jacinta and her friends arrived at Emerald Ridge Weddings. "I'm so delighted to meet you in person." The planner gestured and one assistant came over with flutes of champagne and another whisked away wet umbrellas. "We're going to have so much fun today!"

As the group pushed into the bridal salon, Jacinta tried to focus. By the time Micah had texted her about the theft at the Wellington Ranch, she's heard about the incident from two of her coworkers. "They tied someone up!" one of the salesmen had said. "It's escalating."

That there had been violence frightened Jacinta. Micah could be harmed trying to stop the person. She'd texted him to be careful, and he'd sent back a casual I will, which didn't ease her worry. While she wanted to ask Vivienne for more information, the afternoon's dress shopping appointment was not the time.

Instead, as the wedding planner introduced Jacinta to her sales consultant, Jacinta forced herself to relax. She wanted her family and friends to have fun, especially after the consultant asked Jacinta's bridesmaids and grandmother their opinions on the type of gown they thought suited her, and everyone had answered with such enthusiasm.

The bridal consultant whisked Jacinta away to a dressing room. She caught Jacinta's gaze in the mirror and gave her a friendly smile. "I know what they all said, but what's your style? Mermaid? Ball gown? Beaded? Lots of bling? What do *you* want?"

"I honestly don't know," Jacinta told her. "I don't want to look like a cake topper. Do not listen to a word my cousin says."

"My job is to listen to you," the consultant reassured and Jacinta immediately liked her. "What is your vision? The day is about you."

"I wanted a simple wedding. It's Texas, it's May and I don't want to be sweating. I'll be nervous enough," Jacinta admitted. "All those people looking at me."

"You're marrying Micah Fortune, so I can understand that. Remember, though, the only person you need to look at is your groom. No one else. He'll be at the end of the aisle waiting for you, so let's find a dress that he can't take his eyes off." The consultant stepped back and surveyed Jacinta's figure. "While I pull some things for you to try on, put on this robe and drink your champagne. I'll be right back."

Five long minutes passed by the time the consultant returned carrying three dresses. Jacinta was scrolling through news reports on the latest theft, and she shoved the phone into her handbag as the door opened. "Let's see what you think of these. Remember, it's hard to tell from the hanger."

But Jacinta already was reaching for a clear plastic bag. "Let me see that one."

"Oh, this dress is gorgeous! It's from this year's collection and it just arrived." The consultant named the designer, a name Jacinta recognized as it was a fashion icon. "Here, let's get you into it…"

Jacinta slid into the strapless gown that showed off her collarbones. Small rectangular lace-appliqué flowers created a stunning geometric pattern that widened toward the bottom of the dress. A sheer, lightweight tulle contrasted with the raised flowers, the pattern becoming more dispersed as it reached the floor-length hem. The dress hugged her body until just below her hips, where the mermaid-style skirt flared, becoming almost partially translucent. Not see-through enough to show much, but enough to hint at her legs.

"Oh my," Jacinta said as the consultant clipped her in. Jacinta loved the dress. It was different and minimalist yet classic. "I don't even want to know what this costs."

Knowing the designer, she guessed the dress was over ten thousand dollars. She turned to see what else was in the clear plastic bags, but the skirt swayed, and Jacinta paused. The dress was the most beautiful thing she'd ever seen. If she was stunned by it, what would Micah think?

"Let's go show everyone your first choice," the consultant said, sensing Jacinta's hesitation. "Mr. Fortune gave you carte blanche. Whatever your heart desires. He's so generous."

"He is." Like Cinderella after her fairy godmother's magic, Jacinta slipped into her heels. As they reached the showroom floor, she lifted the gown so she could step onto the circular dais.

"Everyone close your eyes," the consultant directed.

Jacinta moved into position, standing in the reflection of an oversized three-way mirror that caught multiple angles and views of the dress. She was her own harshest critic and even she could see how beautiful she looked.

"Turn around, Jacinta. Now, everyone open your eyes," the consultant said.

Kim was the first one to speak. "Wow."

"You like it?" Jacinta asked, her fingers tracing the embellishments.

Vivienne was on her feet and came closer. "This is beautiful. The fitted silhouette highlights your figure, while the pattern of lace appliqués creates an elongating effect. It's elegant and refined yet the sheer tulle adds a subtle, ethereal quality and a modern touch of allure. It's perfect on you."

"You could sell gowns," Jacinta teased to hide how overwhelmed she was. Because the truth was, she *felt* gorgeous. She turned to the mirror again to get another look.

Vivienne's face came into view in the mirror. "Just because I'm a ranch foreman doesn't mean I don't have a girly soft side. You've met my mother. I might live in jeans and boots, but she made sure I could go from the barn to the ballroom."

"It's breathtaking," Katie said. "I don't even know what else to say."

"I'm still speechless," Carolyn agreed. "You're a bride."

"It's…" The consultant told everyone the designer. "No one in Emerald Ridge will have worn this gown yet. And it fits so perfectly already. The alterations will be a breeze."

"She should try on other things," Sofia said. She drained her champagne. "No one buys the first dress they try on."

"They do if it's a designer worn by first ladies and princesses," Kim snapped back. "Jacinta, what do you think? You could put your hair in a French knot at the base of your neck." Her friend glanced at Sofia as if daring the beauty salon owner to disagree. "You could tuck a small veil into the knot. Not that you need a veil. The dress speaks for itself. You could use a jeweled clip instead."

Jacinta studied herself. The timeless yet contemporary gown combined classic bridal elements like the lace and a strapless silhouette with modern touches like the sheer skirt and geometric lace pattern. She spun around and looked at the one person whose opinion mattered most. "Abuela. What do you think?"

Her grandmother dabbed her cheeks and eyelashes to blot the free-flowing tears. "Your parents would be so proud. I'm proud. You're beautiful, *mi querida*. This is your gown. He won't be able to take his eyes off you."

Jacinta felt her eyes brim as well. It was foolish to spend such an enormous amount on a dress she'd wear once, but she'd never felt so beautiful and fashionable. She didn't want to let Micah down, and she wanted him to gape with awe, and dare she say it, *love*, when she came down the aisle. "Then I'm saying yes to the dress."

Her friends surrounded her and squealed their joy. Kim handed Jacinta more champagne and, once the choice of the bridal gown was settled, the search for bridesmaids' gowns began in earnest. The planner also suggested Jacinta find a going-away gown, and she picked out white midi dress that came with a matching wrap.

Her attendants' dresses ended up coming from the same designer's bridal collection, but instead of floor-length gowns, the cocktail dresses came to just below the knee and featured spaghetti-strap bodices with sweetheart neck-lines. The dresses featured bandana-style floral cutouts edged with silver and white embroidery, with the pattern getting larger as the skirt flared out from the waist. "These are perfect," Vivienne gushed as the girls twirled and the seamstress took their measurements. "The azure blue color of the fabric reminds me of Texas bluebonnets. We should wear silver shoes."

Only Abuela didn't have a dress, but when Jacinta brought it up, she waved off the offer to look for one. "I know what I want," she said. "And it's not here. Don't worry about me."

"Okay." Jacinta hoped Abuela didn't wear the same dress she'd worn to Sofia's nuptials. "But you know I'll shop with you if you want."

"I've been dressing myself a long time," Abuela scoffed

and, with that, the matter was settled. Speaking of settled, Jacinta discovered that Vivienne had paid the bill for everyone's dresses, including the bridesmaids'.

"We're so excited to have you in the family," Vivienne said as she pocketed a receipt whose total must be enough to buy a midsized sedan. "Micah said for you and your friends to get whatever you wanted and not to worry, so you're not worrying." Vivienne leaned over to whisper in Jacinta's ear. "Just kiss him and show him your thanks when you see him next. And I'll help, because later this week I'm taking you shopping for some fancy underthings. I want my brother to be drooling when he gets you alone."

"You know this isn't real," Jacinta reminded her. Although, when she'd seen herself in her dress how she'd wished otherwise. What would it be let loose the growing feelings she had for Micah and perhaps have him love her in return?

As if reading her mind, Vivienne gave her a wink. "You both keep telling yourselves that this isn't real, but the heart has a way of making up its own mind." Vivienne clapped her hands, getting everyone's attention. "All right, everyone, we have another stop to make before we call it quits for the day. Who wants to go sample some dinner entrées? The caterer set out a tasting spread for us, so let's go eat!"

Vivienne took Jacinta's arm and, caught up in the excitement, Jacinta let her soon-to-be sister-in-law sweep her along.

Chapter Eleven

By the time Micah crawled into bed Wednesday morning, his body ached in ways that he hadn't felt in ages. The previous night he'd told Jacinta about his day cleaning tack and how the search the night before had been a bust. He been listening to her melodic voice talk about how she'd found the perfect dress when fatigue had him closing his eyes. Whatever she'd said next had been lost as he'd literally fallen asleep while talking to her. When he'd awakened around 2:00 a.m. for his watchman shift, he'd found a text that said, Hope you had pleasant dreams. We'll talk tomorrow. Hope you catch the guy.

Somewhat embarrassed that he'd dozed off, but grateful she'd understood, he'd shoved the phone in his pocket, grabbed his hat and boots and snuck through the darkened common area. He dressed quickly and exited the bunkhouse onto ground still damp from the day's constant rain. While the precipitation had finally stopped, the downpour had done little to cut the humidity, which hung in the air like a soggy blanket. Tonight he was patrolling with Drake, and he found his brother outside the corral. Drake handed Micah the same shotgun he'd used the previous night.

"How'd things go today?"

Micah slapped at back of his neck to fend off some bug.

"Besides needing to schedule a ninety-minute deep-tissue massage?"

"That bad?"

"Worse. I was so tired I fell asleep talking to Jacinta."

Drake chuckled low. "Ouch. You'll have to make that up to her."

Micah tilted his neck to try to loosen the stiffness. "I work out every day, but ranch work can't be replicated in the gym. However, she told me she bought a wedding dress, so that's good. Vivienne texted me that I'm going to love it."

"You're sure going all-out for a woman you profess you'll divorce in a year," Drake pointed out.

"We're Fortunes, brother. When it's your turn, I guarantee you'll do the same." Micah rested his foot on the bottom slat of the corral fence. "Did Vivienne or Shane see anything while patrolling?"

"Nothing but some bats and a raccoon or two."

"The wrong type of bandit." Micah circled his neck again. "We should probably make our rounds."

"Oh, Vivienne got us these. She said you wouldn't let her be alone last night, so this was her solution." Drake dug into his shirt pocket and removed a small walkie-talkie. "The channel's already set. Call me if you see anything. I'll start on the western side of the stables."

"I'll take the indoor corral and the tack room." The indoor corral/tack room building consisted of multiple wings, and the two men split up.

Unlike the previous night, the soupy air made the long-sleeved black fabric stick to his skin. The disguise didn't help as the wig made perspiration bead on his forehead and the prosthetic nose started to itch. Micah moved slowly and quietly, occasionally crossing the path of a scurrying possum and one of their ear-tipped barn cats. But when he keyed in the code to the exterior tack room door, he frowned. He should have heard a sharp beep indicating he'd deactivated the alarm. Instead, the device had made a deeper sound. He lifted the walkie to his lips. "Drake, tack door alarm's off."

"On my way."

Micah didn't wait. He cracked the door and slid through. Then found himself standing in the dim light of the stable's common room, which was filled with high-top tables and several couch-and-love-seat combinations. Designed to be a gathering spot before and after riding, one interior wall contained a long window overlooking the indoor corral. The red exit lights illuminated enough of the common room and the corral, showing Micah that whoever might be in the stables was not in either space. He eased through the open interior door and into the central corridor. The smell of horse and sweet hay hit his nose.

Each of the stable wings had wash bays, stalls, feed storage and tack rooms. The walkie crackled and Micah held it to his ear. His brother was coming from the opposite side and hadn't seen anything untoward like a trailer, so unless the guy was riding a horse out, he was after something else.

That left the tack room, and instinct told Micah that's where the thief was headed. While certain areas were set aside for the guest tack and worker tack, one part of the stables was private and personal to the Fortunes themselves. Shane, who'd already lost his precious horse, had recently purchased three, high-end Western saddles created just for his build. Whereas Micah liked cars, Shane had thought nothing of spending four or five figures on custom, hand-crafted saddles.

No way was he letting his cousin suffer another loss.

Awake horses nickered as Micah passed, but he ignored them. Up ahead, the low glow of the safety lights illuminated a narrow flat cart sitting outside the tack room door. Two saddles were stacked on top. Shotgun in hand, he strode forward, his footsteps muffled by the rubber mat flooring system that lined the corridors.

A large man stepped out holding a saddle. "Toby? What the hell. You scared me."

For some reason, Micah found himself relieved not to see Rowdy, like he'd expected. The man had made no secret of his needing money for his own place. "Chance. Whatcha doing?"

"Couldn't sleep. Decided to get a jump on tomorrow's work. We never got to these today."

The explanation was logical, but something about the way Chance shifted his weight had Micah sizing him up. The two men were about the same height and build. "I don't know if the Fortunes will like that," Micah said as he eased forward.

Chance shrugged. "Gotta get ahead, man. Need to stand out to get something permanent around here."

Micah had read the employment files of every hired man on the ranch. Nothing about Chance's had created red flags. "Tell you what, it's late. Let's put 'em back and I'll help you clean them tomorrow."

The other guy shook his head as he set the saddle on the cart. "Can't do that. Don't even know why you're here." As Chance straightened, Micah saw a hint of metal in the man's hand before the knife went flying. Micah ducked as the blade sailed by his ear, his movement causing the shotgun to slip and fall to the ground. Thankfully, the knife blade stuck into the wooden stall door and hadn't gone into the stall itself. Before Micah could retrieve the gun, Chance launched forward and tackled him to the ground.

He saw stars and twisted to shake off the man on top of him. Dirt and bits of straw poked his exposed skin. As Chance's fist arced, Micah turned his head and the wrangler's blow glanced off his cheek. Micah winced as the blood came, caused from Chance's ring, which had torn through Micah's flesh. That trigged the muscle memory of having wrestled in high school, which flooded back as if it had been yesterday instead of a decade and half later. He began to fight back and the two men grappled and rained blows, until Micah found an opening and shoved the back of Chance's head against the ground. The man was temporarily stunned, which allowed Micah to clamber to his feet and grab the gun. He turned the shotgun onto a recovering Chance and cocked it. "Don't even think about it," he warned, watching in relief as Chance lowered his head onto the mat and groaned.

Drake ran up. "Are you all right?"

Micah wiped the blood onto his sleeve. "Yeah. Tell the police to come in unmarked cars. He's not going anywhere."

Drake made the call on his cell phone. "They're on their way. Give me the gun and go wash that cut. Might need to be looked at."

Chance watched the exchange with interest. "Toby, who the *hell* are you?" he asked.

Despite the fact the adrenaline was wearing off and the sharp pain was beginning to spread and make him woozy, Micah still managed a grin as he wiped off the blood with the back of his hand. "Me? I'm you're worst nightmare."

Micah didn't return to the bunkhouse that night. Once the police arrived and collected the evidence and carted

Chance away, Micah went to his own home, shed his disguise and crawled into bed. He would have gone straight to the police station, but the officer making the arrest had told them that Chance would not be bonding out any time soon because he'd be facing multiple charges, including attempted murder. For the night, he'd be safe and secure in his locked cell in the Emerald Ridge jail.

Sporting a swollen cheek with a butterfly-shaped bandage holding the cut together, Micah met Vivienne, Drake and Shane at eight the next morning. Too on edge to sit, they stood in a police station conference room with Detective Ebert, who was in charge of the case.

"He's not giving us anything," Detective Ebert told them. "We lifted his prints from the knife and got his real name. His alias was well developed, which is how you didn't know you had a criminal in your midst. He's got a rap sheet a mile long for things like assault, burglary and petty theft."

"Great." Vivienne shook her head, sarcasm clear. Her anger radiated. "I can't believe he'd go so far as to fake his identity. What is the world coming to? We'll need to add fingerprinting to our background checks."

"Shh," Micah said, giving her a comforting side-arm hug. "We're going to get to the bottom of this." He turned to Detective Ebert. "I want to speak with him."

The man frowned. "That's highly irregular. He's asking for his lawyer. We're expecting the guy to show up soon. Answered on first ring. Pretty pricey one, too."

That fact, plus a strong alias, indicated that the thefts and sabotage had to have a puppet master, someone with an agenda who controlled the strings. The ranches were being deliberately targeted.

"I'm the one pressing charges. Let me see what I can do," Micah said. "We want to know why this is happening."

"And where my horse is," Shane added.

"It's worth a try as long as you don't do anything to jeopardize our case," Detective Ebert said. "But I can't be involved in questioning him."

"I'll speak to him alone."

Chance was the only one inside the cellblock, and satisfied the cameras had been shut off, Micah stood in the corridor and looked at the man who wore a bright orange jumpsuit and shoes without laces. "Chance. An appropriate cover name as that's what I'm going to give you."

"Micah Fortune. Should've guessed. Nice little shiner you got." Micah noted Chance no longer had his ring. That would be locked away with his other possessions.

"Tell me what I want to know, Chance, and I'll make life easier on you. Maybe some of your time for my shiner might come off."

The jerk had the gall to laugh. "No can do."

Micah stared at him. "I told you last night I'll be your worst nightmare. I'm not the type of man you want to cross. Why were you stealing saddles?"

Chance shrugged. "I was going to clean them."

"Which is why you threw a knife at me? No one's buying that, dude. You're charged with attempted murder and assault in addition to attempted burglary. You're looking at real time, especially when added to the fact you've violated your probation."

Chance grew angrier. "Look, Fortune, just leave me alone. Ain't telling you nothing."

"Where's our horses?" Micah asked.

Chance folded his arms across his chest. "As I said, I ain't saying nothing else."

Micah decided to try a different tactic. "Give me the

name of who paid you to steal the saddles. That's what we want. I can drop the charges if you help me."

"Can't," Chance said, his answer confirming that he had been paid by someone. He turned his face to the wall. "Go away."

Micah stood there another three minutes, but seeing that the perp wasn't going to spill any secrets, he returned to the detective. When the cameras came back on, they could see Chance on the monitor, lying down with his hands behind his head.

"Get anything out of him?" the detective asked.

"Just that someone paid him to steal the saddles. Whoever it is must be paying him well if he's willing to go to jail for this."

"We'll get to the bottom of it," the detective said as they returned to the conference room. After a quick debrief, the Fortunes left.

When they were in the parking lot, Vivienne pointed at Micah's cheek. "You need to get yourself to a doctor and have him stitch that," Vivienne said. "What's Jacinta going to think if that scars? They'll have to edit your wedding photos."

"Yes, ma'am," Micah said, but because he loved his sister and because the pain hadn't lessened, he did what she'd said and went to urgent care. The doctor had shaken his head, cleaned the wound, and added three stitches that he'd advised could be removed in five days.

While the stitches would be visible for the weekend's charity gala and Mother's Day, he'd been told the swelling should be gone by Jacinta's graduation ceremony. As for their wedding? The doc wouldn't give a guarantee. Micah texted Jacinta he was fine and staying out on the ranch the rest of the week instead of coming into the office. He told her they'd gotten the guy—or they hoped they had, as the Fortunes had no idea if Chance had been part of a group or working alone.

Jacinta had called him immediately after the first text and Micah hated the worry he heard in her voice. Her concern had lessened by Thursday night, at least until he'd finally let her see his face during a video call. Once she'd calmed down and he'd promised that he'd never worry her again, she'd told him that she'd found a dress at the Yellow Rose Boutique to wear to the charity gala.

He'd enjoyed listening to her excitement as she'd told him about the boutique's French Provincial décor and how the faint scent of mimosa had filled the air while she'd shopped. Micah liked being able to give her this type of shopping experience. He could afford to pamper her, and she deserved it. Tomorrow, Vivienne would take her to the spa.

Friday, still battered but feeling better, Micah sat in ranch office. He'd see Jacinta tonight as she was using his kitchen to work on a chocolate recipe. Not only was he excited about seeing her work, but he'd missed her. Had enjoyed their conversations when he'd been undercover and had so many things he wanted to share.

"Micah? *Micah!*" Jarred from his thoughts, he saw Vivienne waving a hand before his face. "I've been calling you for ten minutes."

"Sorry." He knew it hadn't been that long. He sat at the conference table, his cursor blinking in the open document on his laptop.

"Seriously, you've got it bad for her," Vivienne said.

"I was thinking of the ranch," Micah fibbed.

Vivienne's heavenward expression showed she didn't buy that excuse one bit. "Come on. You'll see her later. Right now, our buyer is here."

* * *

Micah was running late. He'd told Jacinta he'd meet her by five, but at six thirty, she still hadn't seen him. He'd sent a text that his meeting had run over. His tardiness had one benefit. She had full run of his lovely, high-end kitchen. Upon first arrival, she'd felt overwhelmed, but then she'd reminded herself that on Monday she'd live here. The door code and the alarm code had worked correctly. When she'd crossed from the foyer into the kitchen, her footsteps had echoed in the still house. Since she didn't know how to work his speakers, music blared from her phone to fill the gigantic space.

She'd brought some of her favorite molds, colorings and tools. Today she was using Columbian cocoa. The process for making Abuela's confections started long before reaching the kitchen. After the cacao pods were harvested, the beans and pulp had to be fermented, dried, roasted, cracked and winnowed to obtain cacao nibs. The nibs were then ground to ensure that the chocolate would feel silky against the consumer's tongue. Once the ground nibs formed a liquor-like paste, the chocolate went through a process called conching to drive out the acidic compounds. Finally, the finished product was tempered.

While her grandmother sometimes still did some of this work by hand, this part of the manufacturing process was mostly performed in a specialized facility that then shipped solid-chocolate bars made to her exact specifications. Abuela melted these bars in a tempering machine and created from there. Since Jacinta didn't have a tempering machine with her, she used a double boiler.

Micah's huge center island made prepping the sunflower molds she was using a breeze. She'd already sprayed inside each mold with bright yellow cocoa butter. One thing her grandmother always insisted on was using natural ingredients. These included the dyes, such as beet juice for coloring things red or spinach for green and carrot for orange colors.

Jacinta had topped the yellow cocoa butter with two layers of chocolate. This would be what the consumer first bit into, so these layers had to have the perfect amount of chocolate. The best candy gave the consumer a satisfying bite before their tongue and teeth hit any ganache filling. Today, Jacinta had made a traditional cream-based, Mexican-vanilla ganache. For an extra kick, she'd added spices to the chocolate itself.

Caught up in her work of piping ganache into the molds, she didn't realize that Micah been watching her for several moments from the mudroom doorway. When she noticed he was there, she jerked her hand, sending filling onto the counter.

"I got it," Micah said. He set his stuff down and grabbed a paper towel. "Sorry to startle you."

"With the music on, I didn't hear you come in." Even with the mark on his cheek, he looked as decadent as the candy she was prepping.

Spill wiped, he threw away the used towel. "I didn't announce myself because you were in the middle of a pretty good song and you were concentrating."

"True." She finished filling the last mold before stirring her melted chocolate. The last step was to pour a final layer of chocolate over the molds and use a flat spatula to scrape off the excess. When inverted, this layer would be the bottom of the candy. Micah reached a finger and swiped a droplet of chocolate that had formed on a countertop covered with waxed paper for easy cleanup. His fingertip slid into his mouth. "Mmm. Delicious. Love the hints of cinnamon. And is that cardamom?"

"It is. I'm impressed." Once poured onto the molds and scraped off, little excess chocolate remained, meaning she'd melted the correct amount. She began to move the filled molds into the freezer. Then turned to see Micah still swiping and eating chocolate from where it had spilled. "That good?"

"Absolutely yes. What did you make?"

"Ganache-filled sunflowers. I can't sell them, since your kitchen, while immaculate, doesn't meet health standards, but I thought I could give a box of them to your mother and your aunt on Mother's Day."

"That's thoughtful." Micah moved to the stove and peered into the top of the double boiler. "She'll love it. This recipe, it's incredible."

"Thanks. I wanted to test a new chocolate idea I had. Abuela doesn't usually use Columbian cocoa, but I asked our manufacturer to create a small batch. Her recipe, but different cocoa."

He lifted the spoon. "Isn't all cocoa the same?"

"Oh no. It's the same as coffee. Or grapes for wine. Where it's grown gives the cocoa beans different flavors."

"I had no idea." Chocolate beginning to harden slowly dripped from the edge of the spoon, and Micah put his finger under it. He brought the morsel to his lips. "So good. Have you tried it?"

When Jacinta shook her head, he stepped forward and held the spoon out. "You're missing out. Open up."

"I'm more worried about that cut on your face."

He held his hand under the spoon. "It's just a scratch. Doc said it'll be good as new. Come on. Try some. I can't believe you didn't taste this."

Perhaps the temptation in his eyes, when combined with the fact he didn't pressure her further by moving the spoon into her space, was what made Jacinta move forward. She closed the gap and licked the melted chocolate from the end. As she did, his expression changed from amused to heated, and desire hung in the air. He swiped chocolate from the end and brought his finger to her lips, smearing the dark liquid onto the top of her bottom lip. When her tongue darted out to lick off the chocolate, he swiped the spoon into the pan so he could repeat the process. This time his finger slid in between her lips and she sucked the deliciousness from his fingertip.

Neither spoke, but Micah's green eyes reflected the impact. Jacinta stood transfixed as he dipped the spoon again. He swiped and then used his finger to trace her lips and paint them once again with chocolate. A hint of a smile formed, but it vanished quickly as he lowered his head so he could sample the sweetness directly from her lips. The kiss sent her spiraling, until Micah drew back to dip his finger into the chocolate again.

Jacinta had never considered melted chocolate to be an aphrodisiac, but as Micah drew a line of it down her neck, she quivered with longing. His lips followed the line, nipping and kissing before stopping at her collarbone. Then his finger returned to the chocolate, bringing one last sample to her mouth. By this time, the mixture, long removed from the heat, had lost its fluidity. Micah set the pan aside and brought his mouth to hers, and Jacinta's tongue tasted chocolate and need. Never breaking the kiss, he guided her away from the counter. His hand slid upward, plucking the hairnet from her head and letting the ponytail fall free.

Then his hands moved to untie her apron and lift it overhead. Because the day was warmer, Jacinta had worn shorts and T-shirt, and Micah's hand raised the hem so his hands could slide around the bare skin of her rib cage. "I want you," he said between the kisses he planted on her neck. "If you don't want me, tell me to stop."

She'd waited too long for this moment to say no. "What I want is for you to keep going."

"I can do that." Micah scooped her into his arms and carried her upstairs. He set her gently on his bed and followed her down. Their lips fused. Her shirt went first, followed by her bra. With her skin above the waist bared to Micah's hot, hungry gaze, his intake of breath spoke volumes before he lowered his mouth to her breast. As the explosions caused by the workings of his tongue ricocheted, Jacinta ran her hands through his hair. "You are so beautiful," he told her when he moved to her other breast. "Tonight is all about you."

Jacinta discovered he meant it. His touch electrified and short-circuited nerve endings. More sensations ricocheted through her as he loosened the button at her waist and slid the zipper down. Then he eased the fabric over her hips and took his time exploring, his entire focus on her enjoyment.

And enjoy she did. Micah was a skilled lover, but making love to him was far more than that. Something elemental connected them, making the moment transcendent. His fingers worked magic, bringing her to a frenzy long before he placed kisses along her inner thighs and found her core. And his mouth? It brought her to even greater heights. Wave after wave carried her away. *"Micah!"*

She crested over and over as he took her above and beyond. He gave her no respite. Like when eating a chocolate truffle, the first bite whetted the appetite. The second added to the joy. His clothing fell to the floor. His lips planted kisses. "Are you ready?"

Ready? She was on fire. She craved him. But words failed. She nodded instead and watched Micah don protection. He propped himself on his arms and moved over her. His mouth found hers and the deep kiss erased any embarrassment or hesitancy or nervousness about the fact that, the moment he slid into her, everything between them would forever change.

His touch gentle but sure, Micah took his time, until Jacinta, whose wanton body had reached the end of its patience, grabbed his strong, muscular buttocks and drew him downward until he completely filled her. "Greedy," he teased. His lips trailed more kisses and he began to thrust. "Is this what you want?"

"Very much so." Jacinta shifted her hips and met Micah stroke for stroke. Bliss began and built, taking her higher. Loving Micah was like watching a solar eclipse. Moment by moment, the anticipation built. Then, at totality, the protective glasses could come off and one could stare at the circle of light formed from the moon's blocking of the sun. Jacinta had seen a total eclipse once, and she'd been awed by the enormity of seeing something so natural yet majestic and powerful. Those three minutes of soft darkness had been worth the wait.

Joining with Micah was also worth the wait, but unlike an eclipse, they could make love again and again. They could bring each other endless pleasure, like… Her brain lost its thoughts as another climax began. Her concentration ceded to the even larger orgasm powering through her. She quaked and shook as the wave built, her fingers clutching his back as she arched to meet him. He kissed her again, his mouth capturing her cries as they came together.

His kiss gentled and then he held her close as each of them tried to catch their breath as the high ebbed. Slowly, he eased away. "I'll be right back."

Jacinta lifted a hand to indicate she understood, but her arm made it mere inches before flopping to the mattress.

She was as boneless as a limp noodle, she was so satiated. Micah came back to the bed and spooned her. He shifted some covers so that they were underneath, and planted kisses along the back of her neck. "That was…"

Exceptional. Mind blowing. Earth-shattering.

"Uh-huh," Jacinta said before he got any of the words out. Wrapped safely in his arms, she closed her eyes. She didn't open them again until well over an hour or so later, when she awoke as needy as before. She shifted and turned to Micah, whose eyes were open. Despite it having long grown dark, there was enough ambient light to see his smile.

"Hey there," he said.

"Hey," Jacinta whispered back. Emboldened, she reached her hand between his legs. Pleased to find he was hard, she wrapped her fingers around him and began to stroke. He made to kiss her but she put her finger to his lips. "My turn."

She wanted to taste him, to feel him, to *pleasure* him, and he let her, until he could take it no longer and rolled her beneath him again. They lay together afterward, Micah lightly stroking her skin. "Move in with me. Tomorrow. I don't want to wait."

"Me either, but tomorrow I'm going with Vivienne to be buffed and scrubbed for the charity gala."

"Then at least spend the nights here with me, and we'll get most of your stuff on Sunday."

Sunday was Mother's Day, but Jacinta could make that timeline work. She and Sofia were taking Abuela out for lunch, but afterward the day was free until the event at the Fortune mansion. She didn't need to move everything immediately anyway. "Okay."

"Good." Micah gave her a kiss. "Perfect."

As he began to make love to her again, Jacinta decided that, for right now, everything was.

Chapter Twelve

The following week passed like a whirlwind. Jacinta absolutely wowed everyone at the charity gala, and Micah was thrilled to introduce her as his fiancée and have her standing by his side. Even though she'd put her things into the closet in what was technically her bedroom, she spent every night sleeping next to him, sharing his space. Their constant lovemaking gave him a permanent smile, and his sister commented that she hadn't seen him happier. He'd attended Jacinta's graduation and whooped his congrats when she crossed the stage, her diploma held high,

Her grandmother kept Micah at a wary arm's length, especially after Jacinta had moved out. He attributed her attitude as a disapproval of cohabitation before marriage, not that she'd said the words. But it didn't matter, so he didn't ask. Jacinta's business plan was full steam ahead, and after her pitch to Poppy, Jacinta was working on creating an exclusive line of chocolates for the guest ranch and spa. While his bride-to-be hadn't yet given him the go-ahead to invest, he had real estate agents looking for production space for her expansion.

Everything was on track, including the nuptials. Even though he had two custom tuxes, the wedding planner had insisted he needed a new one, so he'd been fitted for another tux. His groomsmen had theirs. The dinner menu was set… He let his mind drift, remembering the cake tasting. He'd held a fork with a portion out and fed it to Jacinta. If they hadn't been in public…suffice to say clothes hadn't stayed on once they'd returned home.

"You're looking pleased with yourself," Drake said. It was the Sunday before the wedding, and Micah's bachelor party was being held in a private room at the Emerald Saloon at the same time Jacinta's bridal shower was occurring out at the Leonetti Vineyards. Neither he nor Jacinta had wanted traditional bachelor-bachelorette events, like a debauched weekend in Vegas. There wasn't time anyway, not with the wedding in seven days. Jacinta had told him yesterday during her graduation dinner at Captain's that she wasn't going to miss having a bachelorette party. "A shower is all I need," she'd said. "And I don't even need that, but my bridal party insisted."

To ensure it was the best shower ever, Micah had told his sister to spare no expense and to give Jacinta a specific gift from him. Vivienne had promised to take pictures and video.

"Earth to Micah," Drake said, waving a hand in front of his face. "I know you're not seriously watching the Stanley Cup playoffs. It's a replay of last night's game anyway. Where's your mind? Your last dart game, you didn't hit the bull's-eye once. Although I can wager a guess why you're so distracted…"

"Sorry." Micah snapped to attention and took a sip of bourbon. "Thinking about everything that has to happen this week. We still don't know who's behind the thefts. The lab still hasn't gotten us the DNA results. I can't believe these are taking longer than expected and…"

"And you're falling in love with your bride." Drake saluted him with a longneck.

"No." Micah's denial came fast and hard.

Drake held back a laugh. "I've known you all my life. Fortune blood might not be running through my veins—"

"That's never mattered," Micah interrupted, not understanding why Drake was even bringing it up now. Drake had been adopted as a newborn, when Micah was young. One of his earliest memories was of his parents bringing home his new baby brother. Somewhere his twenties Micah had learned the reason for the adoption was that his mom had had a miscarriage and his parents had still wanted more children. "You are as much of a Fortune as I am," Micah insisted to Drake.

"I know that, so if you'd let me finish, I was going to say we're as close as two brothers can be, even more so than some blood brothers. In this case, I'd say I know you better than you know yourself. You're falling in love with her. It's evident to all of us how happy she makes you."

"It's a business deal," Micah said stubbornly. But before Drake could protest, friends joined them, effectively ending the conversation, much to his relief. By becoming lovers, he and Jacinta had already moved the goalposts once. Micah refused to let them be moved again.

"Thank you everyone," Jacinta said. She sat on a chair surrounded by stacks of unwrapped presents. Overwhelmed, tears threatened. "This is all so much. Everyone's been so kind and generous. I'm flattered and so grateful."

"There's one more." Her grandmother approached, holding a long and thin rectangular box.

Jacinta set down the champagne glass. "Abuela. You didn't have to give me anything."

"But I did," her grandmother said.

She carefully unwrapped the ribbon, but it broke, eliciting cries of "That's another one. What are you up to, Jacinta? *Three kids?*"

Jacinta laughed with her guests and handed the broken ribbon to Poppy, who strung it through the paper plate she was using to make Jacinta's rehearsal bouquet. While she might not be having a bachelorette party, her bridal party had insisted that some shower traditions were too important to forgo.

She slid her finger under the pretty silver paper and removed a white box. Suspecting what was inside, her fingers trembled as she lifted the lid. Inside lay the signed legal paperwork transferring Abuela Rosa Chocolates into her care.

"Abuela." Jacinta handed Vivienne the box and rose to embrace her grandmother. *"Te amo mucho,"* she said. "So much," she added in English, wanting to express how much she loved her grandmother. *"Gracias."* She turned to the crowd gathered there. "Abuela just gave me her company."

Everyone clapped, even Sofia, a fact for which Jacinta was grateful. She hugged and kissed her grandmother again. "Thank you," she whispered in her ear. Abuela had surprised her by not waiting until after the wedding, like Jacinta had expected.

"I love you," Abuela spoke in English so everyone would understand. "I'm proud of the woman you've become. Your parents would be, too."

"Aww," the crowd said as the two women again embraced.

"This has meant so much." Jacinta pushed aside the guilt that crept in at the fringes.

After additional toasts, Vivienne stood. "There's one last gift." She handed Jacinta a small square box wrapped in satin ribbon and a large center bow. "This one's from Micah."

"Okay." The box was the size to hold bracelets or a neck-lace, so once she lifted the lid, Jacinta hadn't been expect-ing to find a car key fob inside. She dangled it from her finger. "Vivienne…"

"Outside everyone for a moment." Her future sister-in-law led the way outside, where at the entrance to the win-ery a shiny, brand-new, dark blue crossover covered with a big white bow waited.

"He got me a car." Jacinta pressed the fob and the doors unlocked. She couldn't quite believe this. "He bought me a car…"

Vivienne's grin covered her entire face. "Now you know why I insisted on driving you today. And let's face it, that old car you were driving was on last legs. Now get in so I can take some pictures for Micah and then we'll go back inside. We still have cake to eat."

Jacinta climbed onto the driver's seat and ran her fin-gers over the leather-wrapped steering wheel. The vehicle was fully loaded and had every amenity, including leather seating and a sunroof. Micah was so generous, as a man, a lover and friend. Soon he'd be her husband. She smiled for the pictures and blew Micah a kiss in the video Vivi-enne recorded.

"You certainly won the jackpot," Sofia said later as the party wrapped and guests began to leave. "He must love you very much."

Jacinta couldn't utter the words that voiced the lie that Micah had no such feelings, so she nodded instead. Vivi-enne had overheard the conversation, and she came and threw her arm over Jacinta and faced Sofia. "Of course he does. She's the light of his life."

Jacinta turned toward Vivienne and shot her future sister-in-law a warning glance. Vivienne's chin jutted forward. "You are," she said the moment no one could overhear them. "Both of you need to realize you're perfect for each other. Let's load up your new car and get this stuff back to your place."

Jacinta arrived to the house first—despite Vivienne's words, she couldn't yet think of it as her "home"—and Micah's sister helped her unload and unpack the presents. Jacinta knew he would want to see things, so she left out the practical items. She tucked the lingerie, which had seemed to be a common gift theme, in a dresser drawer in her bedroom. She glanced at the bed she hadn't used since moving in. Overwhelmed, she sat on the edge. What was she doing? Why wasn't she over the moon with joy?

Because, if she were honest with herself, she was falling for Micah. No, "falling" wasn't the right word. She was *in love* with him. If this were a marriage based on love, life would be wonderful. But it wasn't and a tiny piece of her heart splintered.

Hearing the garage door open, she went downstairs to find Micah walking into the kitchen. "Hey, I see you drove your new car. How do you like it?"

"It's wonderful," Jacinta said as he drew her into his arms. "Thank you."

Micah tugged her close and she lost herself in his kiss until she heard a cough. Drake stood there with boxes in his hand. "Where do you want this stuff?" he asked.

"Kitchen table is fine," Micah said, never loosening his grip on her. "Looks like there are some gifts over there already."

"We have so much stuff to go through," Jacinta said once

Drake had left and after the two readjusted clothing lost during a quick coupling on the great room sofa.

She pointed to the stack of presents. "This is why we didn't do a registry. Can't we just tell people to donate to charity instead of giving us wedding gifts?"

"We can suggest it, but we also can't rob them of the joy of gifting. If we can't use it, we'll find a good charity and donate whatever we don't want. There are plenty places eager for household items and such."

That satisfied her. "Oh, Abuela gave me these." She handed him the papers.

"Already?" He was as shocked as she'd been.

Jacinta nodded. "Yeah. Surprised me, too. But it's mine."

"Great. Then I can't wait to invest." Micah began to outline the ways his money could be used, until Jacinta put her hand up.

"We're moving too fast. I don't want your money right now. Let's talk about the business next week, once the wedding is behind us."

"Is there something wrong?" Micah's brow furrowed, his gaze searching hers.

She searched for the right words, for telling him she loved him was not an option when he wouldn't reciprocate her growing feelings. "Today was hard. Everyone is so happy for us. They think this is a love match and I hate duping them about our true reasons for tying the knot. My conflicting feelings are causing me stress."

"It's a real marriage," Micah reminded her. He pushed his hair off his forehead, the cut on his cheek having lost its angry lump and redness. "You and I get along great and we have incredible sex. It's probably better that we don't have feelings. Those get in the way. Set unrealistic expectations."

"I can't believe that," she said. "I know you were hurt before, but I'm not *her*."

His gaze narrowed. "I never said you were."

"I know." She didn't want to fight. There was no point in telling him she loved him. He wouldn't return the words. She accepted the kiss he gave her, letting herself get lost in the chemistry they shared as clothing again flew. She could at least have his lovemaking over the next year. Maybe, if she were lucky, he might change his mind and open his heart to her.

Maybe she truly would have it all.

Jacinta kept those hopeful thoughts front and center as she walked down the aisle at the wedding. From the over-whelming expression of awe and desire registering on Micah's face, as she came down the white runner toward him wearing her wedding dress, Jacinta could almost believe that he loved her. She kissed Abuela goodbye and turned to him.

"You look gorgeous," he said, taking her hands in his. "This dress. Wow. I'm speechless. You have completely made me come undone."

A lump formed in her throat. The dress had had the impact she'd wanted, the result he'd requested. "You don't look so shabby yourself."

His grin widened and the beginning of the ceremony went by in a blur. Vivienne had planned the ultimate wedding, converting an outdoor space on the ranch into a flower-covered arboretum. Mother Nature had blessed the Fortunes yet again, this time with perfect weather for an outdoor ceremony.

"Our couple has written their own vows," the celebrant said. "Micah?"

Her hands secure in his, Micah gazed into her eyes. "Jacinta, you came into my life like a whirlwind, making my days in the office bright and fabulous. You found a part of me I didn't know I was missing, and for that I will be forever grateful. I never thought I'd marry, and now I can't imagine marrying anyone but you. You're my other half, the one who brings out the best in my heart and soul. I am overjoyed you've chosen me as your husband, especially because I know I don't deserve you. I promise I will cherish and honor you to the end of our time together, enjoying the moments our life together brings. My bride, will you take me as yours?"

Jacinta tried to keep the tears away. While everyone would hear Micah's words as proof of their love, Jacinta knew they were perfectly crafted for show. Not once had he actually said he loved her. He hadn't even alluded "until death do us part." He'd threaded the needle in his perfect Micah way, telling her how much he cared for her and how important she was.

"Jacinta?" the celebrant prompted.

"Yes." She blinked and smiled at her groom. Micah appeared so tall and solemn in his tux. She was glad her four-inch stilettos gave her some height. "Micah, my beloved." For that was true. She couldn't help herself. In her vows she had to speak the truth.

"I agonized over what to say to you. How do I tell you my feelings about everything you've done for me and how you make me feel? That it's more than simple gratitude that you came into my life. That you complete me and make my dreams come true? Elizabeth Barrett Browning once said, 'Let me count the ways.' I tried and realized that even her declaration of love wasn't enough, that the number of ways was infinite. So I ask you to take care of my heart. Will you do that for me?"

She'd shocked him, but Micah recovered quickly. He gave her a strong "I will" before kissing her soundly.

The wedding officiant laughed and shouted over the guests' cheers, "I pronounce you husband and wife," and Jacinta and Micah surfaced for air when the celebrant announced them, saying, "Honored guests, may I introduce the newly married Micah and Jacinta!"

The kissing didn't stop during the reception either, with knives clinking on glasses demanding more kisses. Vivienne had decorated one of the older barns so that the venue combined rustic charm with modern, luxurious accompaniments. The reception played host to a crowd of two hundred. Dinner was barbecued steaks, chicken breasts and lobster tails served with a multitude of sides, including four types of rolls, various hot and cold salads, mashed and baked potatoes, honey-glazed carrots and almondine green beans. The wedding planner had called the menu "elevated comfort food," and as a server cleared her plate, Jacinta admitted her meal had been delicious. The James Beard award–winning chef had outdone himself.

Jacinta and Micah cut the first slice of a four-tier cake so the caterers could take it away and plate it. They danced their first dance together, and Micah had whispered in her ear the entire time how much he wanted to undo the buttons running down her back. After their dance, their guests took to the dance floor. Over the course of the evening, Jacinta met so many people that she couldn't keep track of everyone—getting an invitation to a Fortune wedding had been a coveted event. She was grateful when her grandmother approached and began chatting.

"Did I tell you how much I love your dress?" Jacinta

asked. Abuela had found a perfect gray-silk dress that Jacinta knew hadn't been in her closet.

"Thank you. Where are you honeymooning? I don't think you ever told me."

"We're waiting," she told her. "Micah has some business dealings that he can't get out of." She didn't elaborate about the thefts and sabotage. "I'm also ready to take over and implement some of my business ideas."

"Once things settle, I'm taking her to Europe this fall for an extended trip." Micah appeared and slid his arm around his bride. "I'd prefer to go when it's not overrun with tourists."

"That makes sense," Abuela said. "And tonight...?"

Micah held Jacinta close and brushed his lips over her temple. "Is a secret, but we won't be on the ranch."

"Good." This seemed to satisfy her grandmother. She gazed at him and nodded her approval. "I can tell you love her very much. It's all I've ever wanted for her, to be happy like I was and like her parents were."

"We're very happy," Micah assured her.

Jacinta glanced over her shoulder to avoid her grandmother's sharp gaze. "Oh look, they're serving cake."

Grateful to escape, she threw herself into trying to enjoy the remainder of the reception. She danced with her friends, danced with Micah and drank way too much champagne. Then it was time to change into her going away dress, and sparklers lit up the night as their guests formed a line to the awaiting limo. The doors closed and their driver drove off into the night.

Jacinta leaned back in her seat. She and Micah were finally alone. "Where are we going? And you have my bag, right?"

"I do and it's a surprise." Micah reached for her hand.

Jacinta glanced out the window as they reached the Emerald Ridge airport. The limo drew alongside a private plane sitting on the tarmac. As the driver opened their door, the stairs descended, and a pilot appeared. She craned her neck. "What's this? This really is a surprise." He was constantly doing these sweet things for her. Maybe his romantic gestures could mean his heart would soften?

He grinned. "Come on. It's not a long flight. Not long enough for us to do anything fun." Micah guided Jacinta aboard the luxurious jet as the driver transferred their luggage to the plane.

The flight took forty minutes and, once on the ground, Micah ushered her into a waiting car. He drove them twenty minutes from the airport to a beautiful lakeside house. While she couldn't see the water because of the darkness, the sky above was brilliant with a million stars. "What is this place?"

"It's my retreat." Micah told her. "It's where I come when I want to get away, maybe do a little boating and fishing. Now it's our bolt-hole. Our personal getaway. Minus my family, you will be the first woman I've ever brought here." He lifted her into his arms and carried her across the threshold and straight upstairs. "I hope you like it. I promise to show you the rest, but right now, I want to get you out of this dress."

Sex was common ground, and as her future as his wife began tonight, Jacinta went with the flow. "Sounds like a plan."

Long after Jacinta had fallen asleep, Micah rose and walked out onto the balcony. Everything about the day had been perfect—the dress, their first kiss as a married couple, the reception, the food, the band. *Perfect*. He was happy.

Content. Only one thing kept him from being one hundred percent satisfied. She loved him. He'd felt the change tonight in their lovemaking. He'd heard the words in her vows. Being in love wasn't part of the plan.

"Micah?"

"Over here. Did I wake you?" He'd thought her worn out from their copious lovemaking.

"What's wrong?" Barefoot and wearing a silky scrap of fabric that immediately made him hard, she joined him. The reflection of the late-rising moon created a rippling path along the water. "The moon's out."

"Yeah." His lower half gladly reacted to her presence, tenting the front of his boxers. Would he ever get enough of her? Did he even want to?

She placed her hand on his forearm. "You couldn't sleep?"

"Maybe just the excitement of the day. It was a great wedding and reception. Everyone told me how wonderful it was. I admit, I was worried how things would go."

"What do you mean? I don't understand."

He had to nip her budding feelings before they bloomed fully. "Well, it's a real marriage. But I was afraid my closed heart might give me away as a man who doesn't believe in love. But we pulled it off. Everyone believed this is a love match."

"Yes, they did."

The night's shadows concealed her face, but Micah heard the hurt in her tone. He'd wounded her. He hated doing it, but he couldn't let Jacinta get fanciful ideas that their marriage was anything more than what it was. "I'm glad I was able to give you a perfect day."

"It's one I won't forget." Her upbeat tone had flattened.

She shivered and he became concerned she might catch cold. He scooped her into his arms and carried her to the bed. "Let's get you back inside where it's warmer and not so damp."

"Okay." When she reached for him, Micah kissed her like the world might end tomorrow.

"You know I don't want to hurt you," he said in between kisses. "You know this is all I can give you."

"I know." She slid her lips down the side of his neck. "I'll take what I can get."

Micah knew she'd forced the answer, so he worked to bring her pleasure. He might not be able to offer her a traditional marriage, but he *could* ensure she was satisfied.

The next morning, he cooked her breakfast and brought her a steaming mug of hot chocolate. He set his own mug down as he took a seat. "I made it using your Abuela's recipe. I hope I did it justice."

Jacinta's eyes closed in momentary pleasure. "Micah, this is perfect. Thank you."

"I wanted to do something special for you. I'm not always the best at expressing my feelings, but I'm trying. I know I said I can't give you my heart, but the more time I spend with you, the more I realize how much you do mean to me. It's not easy for me to let people in, but I do want to try to be the best husband I can be. I can give you that. Please allow me to do that."

"I'd like that," she said, giving him a smile he felt in his toes.

After breakfast, he showed her around the property before initiating another round of lovemaking. By the time they flew home late on Memorial Day, he'd lost count of how long they'd stayed in bed. He knew he had to be careful, as she was the type of woman a man could fall for. If only he weren't so damaged. Or jaded. Or far older.

By Tuesday, they were back in the office. As the place

took up an entire floor and he didn't seek her out, he didn't see her until lunch. By then, they were both hungry for something other than food, so he'd locked the door and ravished her. He'd been unable to help himself. He'd missed her. He refused to consider why.

They were in the middle of eating actual food when his phone chimed with multiple text messages. Micah set his sandwich down. "That's my family's group thread. Something must have happened." He swiped open the phone. "Oh no. *Damn it*."

"What's wrong?" Midbite, Jacinta set her sandwich on the red-and-white-checkered wrapper.

"Poppy just texted. The DNA results for Jennifer Johnson finally came back from the lab. Jennifer is Joey's mother." Micah's fingers began typing a reply to the family. "I can't believe this. She's a grifter, the worst type of human. That poor child. She wants five hundred thousand to walk away. Sorry, I'm venting. The longer it took, the more I hoped…"

"It's okay. She's terrible. I'm sorry your family has to go through this. But if she'll sign over the rights, maybe that's a good thing."

"Hopefully." Micah calmed himself. The hits kept coming. First no progress on who had hired Chance. And now getting proof that Jennifer was Joey's mom? His anger bubbled. "The fact she's willing to give up her baby is the only bright side of this. I still can't believe that, in exchange for a half mil, she'll sign over parental rights and agree to allow Poppy and Leo to legally adopt Joey. The money means nothing. It's a baby. He deserves better. Leo and Poppy love him." He paused to draw breath. "How can she sell her baby? Who would do that? No one but a truly sick and twisted individual."

"I agree. She must be desperate to do such a thing." Jacinta reached over and placed a comforting hand on his arm. "I still believe it will work out okay. Your family will get through this, Micah. You have resources."

"That, we do, and we'll use all of them." He appreciated Jacinta was with him when he'd gotten the news. She radiated sympathy for his family, remaining the calm presence he needed. "Trust me, the family is chatting now. That's the reason my phone is blowing up. We're trying to figure out next steps. We're all disgusted by how our family is essentially being forced to pay for the adoption. Having a child shouldn't be transactional."

Jacinta packed away her lunch. "No, you're right. It shouldn't be. Not at all."

As Micah stared at her strangely, Jacinta shook her head and took her hands off her stomach. "Oh wait. You think… Oh no. Not me. Sorry."

"You had me worried for minute there. Whew."

"Nope. No worries on my account." She'd been on the pill to control her periods for years, and once her doctor had assured her that if she took it correctly she should be safe, she and Micah had stopped using condoms. The three broken ribbons at her shower came into mind, but no, she wasn't pregnant. No chance of that. Besides, while she loved Micah and would love to have his children, she wouldn't bring them into a marriage that was, on his side, transactional in nature. From his expression of relief, it was clear having children with her would never be on the agenda. Her heart splintered further.

Why, oh why had she crossed the line by adding sex into the mix? Why had she let herself believe that he would change? She knew better. But she'd allowed herself to get caught up in the Cinderella fantasy and a dream wedding.

"So what happens next?" Even if he'd never love her, she wanted to support him.

Micah rose and carried his trash to the waste can. "Everyone wants Poppy and Leo to be happy. They've bonded with Joey. Poppy would move the sun, moon and stars to keep him. For the time being, the current plan is to string Jennifer along with the promise of payment until we figure out how best to manage the adoption. We'll want to ensure that Jennifer will really go. If we pay her, it's about making sure she leaves forever and never darkens our doorway again."

Jacinta moved to wrap her arms around him. "It'll be okay. I don't know why I believe that, but I know it will."

He stepped out of her reach, as if the closeness had crossed a line. "Thanks. I appreciate that. I should get back to work. Tonight, though, let's talk about your business. I'm ready to invest and I don't know why you haven't given me the go-ahead to transfer the money. We're married now. That was part of our deal."

"Because…" She faltered. After Micah's reminder of his unattainable heart, the thought of taking his money left a bad taste in her mouth. While he wasn't the devil, and wasn't even close to being one, she still felt as if she'd sold her soul. She'd compromised her values for a marriage of convenience and some great sex so that she could take over Abuela's company and stick it to her cousin. While she'd gone into the situation with eyes wide open, she hadn't considered the ramifications on her psyche, on the guilt she felt and on the despair of knowing she'd fallen in love with the one man who'd never love her back. She was like a novice swimmer realizing far too late that she'd entered a riptide.

Jacinta put on a brave face. "You're already giving me so much that I decided I'm expanding the business myself, without any additional help."

The corner of his lips bent downward as he peered at her. "What do you mean? You need cash and the Realtors are going to bring you a bunch of potential locations this week."

"I mean that if I want money, I'll get a small business loan, like it's written in my business plan." She caught herself before she nibbled her lower lip.

Micah paced. "Look, this makes no sense. We're married. We should be partners in everything."

Jacinta shook her head. Today, once the sun had risen and they'd returned to the office, it was as if the magic had evaporated. Or maybe she'd simply stopped deluding herself that the emperor wore clothes. He'd never love her. Lust yes, but love, no. She was living a lie. She couldn't be with someone who didn't love her. She felt as if she was drowning. Feared becoming become a shadow of her former, confident self. As the time marched onward, she'd love him more and more while he simply bided time until they divorced. She had to regain control.

"Micah, we have to be realistic. This partnership is temporary. The clock began ticking yesterday. Our marriage has an expiration date, so we have three hundred sixty-three days left." She couldn't face the fact that she'd be the ex-wife of Micah Fortune. It wasn't a badge of honor she wanted.

His forehead creased. "I didn't know you were counting."

"Micah, our entire relationship is transactional and physical. My grandmother wanted me to find my soulmate. I have the business thanks to you, but I meant what I said when I made my vows." She took a breath and rushed onward. "I've fallen in love with you. I love you. And I know that's the last thing you want."

And she'd never meant to say it out loud like this, in his office, over lunch. Then again, most of their big decisive moments came during their lunches—his proposal, their first kiss, and her decision she couldn't do this anymore. It was as if the sensible part of her had resurfaced, pushed her head above water into the light and let her breathe again. She had to wrest back control, even if ripping the bandage off her heart to let it bleed would hurt worse than anything.

"I…" He clamped his mouth shut because he couldn't deny what she'd said. He didn't want her love, and sorrow shot through her like an arrow, piercing her deep. "I'm sorry."

Jacinta's shoulders lifted and fell in resignation. "I'm sorry too. I'm the one who fell in love with you, and I knew better. I knew you had a well-guarded wall when it comes to me, but for some reason I hoped I could convince you otherwise. I never should have made that assumption." After all, Cinderella was just a story and princes didn't really fall for their interns.

"Where do we go from here?"

It was a fair question. She'd jumped headlong into this conversation without really thinking it through. But she knew appearances mattered to him, and he had helped her. And he was sweet and kind and thoughtful. He'd wanted to help her.

"If you're worried, I'm not divorcing you until our agreement reaches its term, unless you want something different. But we've muddied the waters, and given my feelings, we should probably put on the brakes."

"Agreed. I don't want to hurt you. That was never my intention."

"I know." But she'd opened herself to the possibility the moment she'd considered the idea of marriage, and doubled down when she'd believed they could be more following lovemaking. For that's what it had been on her side. Which meant that as much as she desired him, she had to stop doing foolish things. While she couldn't put the genie back in the bottle, she could end things to preserve her sanity. She couldn't touch him and know he'd never love her, that for him it was just sex.

"From here out, I think it's best if I move back into my bedroom. We should keep the marriage as you wanted it in the first place—convenient and platonic."

His cheek twitched. "If that's the way you want it."

It was the last thing she wanted, but she'd lose herself if she didn't. Touching him was like eating cake. One bite was never enough. "I do think it's best."

It was actually the worst thing, and she recognized the irony of those words as she determined to survive the year. Hopefully, someday the pain of loving him would pass. Before the tears poured down, she determined to make her escape. "Which means I should also get back to work. I'm going out with my friends tonight, so I'll see you when I get home."

"Oh, Jacinta." It was Kim who provided the first hug when she met her friends for happy hour again on Thursday night. "Are you sure you're doing the right thing? When we saw you Tuesday evening after you told Micah you wanted to keep things platonic, you were miserable. Now you're an absolute mess."

Jacinta tried not to cry, as she'd been doing since the moment she left Micah's office. "I'm a disaster. It hurts. Every day it gets worse. We circle around each other like prizefighters trying to avoid another hit. I want to touch him, but I can't because if I do, then I'm letting my baser urges have free reign. The sexual tension is driving me crazy. I want him. But I can't give in. I love him too much. I don't want to be a bug that keeps flying towards the zapper."

"Has he said anything?" Katie asked.

"We talked again last night. I told him I'm too much in love with him to continue to live this way. I can't do unemotional. So I assume he now thinks of me as a huge mistake."

"Did he say that?" Carolyn patted Jacinta's arm, the motion comforting.

Jacinta summed up the conversation with a simple, "No, not exactly. He admits he's closed off where I'm concerned. He tells me he'll give me anything but his heart. I don't think he understands that I don't care about his money. It's the last thing I want from him."

"I'm truly sorry. You knew this going into it, but that was before everything else," Carolyn said. "You know, the sex part."

"Yeah, believe me, I know. The sex changed everything." Jacinta's lips quivered. "And no, this isn't hormones. You know how short my cycles are and I just finished."

"Never thought it was," Katie said. "We know you."

Jacinta was so stressed she hadn't even touched her glass of wine. If she started drinking she might not stop until she'd numbed the pain, and everyone knew that drinking to excess never solved anything. Problems simply returned along with the ensuing hangover. "I've been wrestling with my decision for two days and don't see any other option than one. I'm going to tell my grandmother the truth tomorrow. I'm giving up the business. It's the right thing to do."

"No! Not to Sofia!" Kim protested. "You can't do that. Your cousin can't win. She'll sell and you know it."

"Yeah, I know, but I can't live like this." Coming to that realization had been one of the most difficult of her life, along with deciding to never touch Micah again if she could avoid it. Jacinta knew it was the right choice, even it was a hard choice requiring heavy, metaphorical lifting.

She reached rubbed a forefinger on the table. "I'd rather live honestly, even if I'm heartbroken over losing both of my loves, Micah and Abuela Rosa Chocolates. I can start something new, move somewhere else. I'll stay in the marriage for the year, as promised, but it's killing me to see him every day. I can't live like this. It breaks my heart to be under his roof."

"We don't want you to leave Emerald Ridge, but if you do, you know we will fully support you," Katie said. "You've got an MBA. Someone will hire you. Let me reach out to my contacts."

"Thanks. I'm also putting out feelers starting Monday. It'll be too awkward to keep working for the Fortunes. I've got some savings, so I'll be fine for a while." Jacinta refused to take a dime of any of the prenup money.

"When are you telling him you're going to leave him?" Carolyn asked.

"Tonight. When I get home. It won't do me any good to wait. The only way I'm going to begin to heal is if I don't have to see him. When he smiles, I simply want to throw myself into his arms."

Kim pointed to Jacinta's wineglass. "Well, if you're about to end your marriage, some liquid courage won't hurt. Girl, you better have some of that wine."

In the end, Jacinta took a total of two sips of wine. Her heart wasn't into drinking and her sour stomach rejected food. It had been a long, gut-wrenching week and it wasn't even over. Before she and her friends left, she ordered carry-out. Micah was working late, and when he arrived, she wanted to have food waiting for him. Besides, it might make things easier for what she had to say if he had a full stomach.

"Hey," he greeted as he entered the kitchen. He made no move to kiss her as he had all those times before she'd told him that she wanted to keep things platonic. For the past several days, he'd also made a concentrated effort to stay in his own space. She hated every minute of it. No, she couldn't continue to live like this, being reminded she would never be loved. She couldn't keep seeing him.

They ate at opposite ends of the kitchen table, separated by six feet of space. "Thanks for ordering food," he said. "How was happy hour?"

She didn't meet his gaze. "It was good to see my friends."

"You just saw them on Tuesday." A forkful of chicken fettucine paused midair.

She had little appetite and used her fork to push her noodles around. "Yes, but I made some decisions between now and then."

"That sounds ominous." He set the fork down, contents intact.

Jacinta sighed and faced him. "Yeah. I can't keep doing this. I can't live with you. Maybe we should put this failed experiment behind us."

His pushed his plate toward the center of the table, most of his meal uneaten. "I believe I heard you say in not so many words that you want to end this." His cheek twitched. "I'd like you to spell it out for me, say the words. Make sure I'm correct and didn't misinterpret your meaning."

"Micah, your family has enough to deal with right now. You have to consider Baby Joey, you still have to find who hired the saboteur and your family doesn't need our marital issues compounding things."

"We've been managing just fine." The chin she'd covered with kisses set in that stubborn way of his.

Maybe they had been, until she'd realized she loved him. "I was wrong when I thought I could give up on love for a year. And I told you how I feel, and I know me loving you is the last thing you want."

He folded his arms across his chest and frowned.

Jacinta pressed on. "Frankly, I deserve to be married to a man who loves me back. I shouldn't have to settle. Someone once told me you have to leap and let the net appear. That's what I'm planning on doing."

"Am I really that horrible?"

She worked to reassure him on that point. "No. Not at all. It's not you. It's me."

"It really feels like it's me. If I loved you, we wouldn't be having any of these issues. You wouldn't be unhappy."

"I'm unhappy because I'm lying to people."

"But it's a real marriage."

"Yes, but not in the way that really matters. Love is what matters. That's what my grandmother wanted for me. I deceived her. And maybe some can rationalize it, but I can't. Not anymore. It's eating me up inside."

A pause stretched before Micah said, "I see."

She worried he didn't. "After work tomorrow, I'm telling my grandmother the truth. If she demands the business back, which I'm quite prepared for and probably will offer anyway, I'll give it to her, even if that means it's going to Sofia. I have to do the right thing. I let myself get off course, off track, swept along in a fantasy. The love, that's real. But this—" she gestured around "—is not. We're too old to play house."

His thumped against the back of the chair and scowled. "You'd give up your dream. Because you want to change the terms of our agreement and bring emotions into it."

"Is it really a dream when I'm having to lie to everyone that we are in love? When I give you my body because I love you and you take it because it's a chemistry thing? That's not a dream I want. I'm sorry that I thought I could. That's on me." Jacinta stood and took her plate into the kitchen and set it on the counter. He was still at the table when she returned, so she sat across from him again. "And yes, I will give up what was my dream, even if that means giving up the company I wanted to be mine. I can't deceive my grandmother."

His face was unreadable, and her heart suffered its final break. "All because I can't love you back?"

"I realized something when I fell in love with you. Life is not about stuff or having tons of money. It's about family and love and being with the person who means the world to you. It's finding your soulmate. When I realized that I loved you, I hoped that you were mine, that fate put us together for a reason, but I'm realizing that's not the case. I'm not being fair to you if I expect you to change. I can only change myself."

She rested her palm on the table, the marble top cool to the touch. "You know how when you were in high school and you were friends with people, and then you drifted apart? People come and go in our lives for a reason. I'll always be grateful for what you've done for me, Micah. More than you know." She swallowed a lump in her throat. "But…when I speak with my grandmother, I'm also going to ask her if I can move home until I figure out my next step. If she agrees, I'll move my stuff out of here on Saturday. I don't expect it will take me too long to land on my feet. Before I left her tonight, Katie told me about a job in Dallas and I'm putting in an application for it on Monday."

His face paled. "You'd leave your job, too? And your business? All because I can't love you? That seems rather drastic."

"Yes. Drastic or not, I am doing just that. I'll stay married to you for the year, if you still want. I'll honor that commitment but nothing more. I'll also leave if you decide that's best." They were some of the hardest words she'd ever had to speak and somehow she managed to do so without breaking. She'd do that later, once she was alone.

"Being my own person and being happy and comfortable in my skin, that's more valuable to me than any business or any job. I can always start another business and find another job. But I believe in love and I *want* love, and a marriage that will last a lifetime. And as much as I wish things were different, I know that I'm not going to have that with you." She bit her lip to divert the tears from forming. "Plus, I'm not getting any younger. On that, my grandmother was right."

He sat there, unable to hide how stunned he was. A variety of expressions fitted across his face, from disbelief to anger, to hurt and resignation. Jacinta had thought her heart was done shattering but she was wrong.

"I hate this," he said.

"So do I."

"And there's nothing I can do?"

"No. Believe me, I wish things were different. I don't know the woman who broke you, Micah, but I wish she hadn't. Since she did, I really wish you'd realize I'm not her. You might think so since I'm leaving you, but if you truly loved me…"

She paused. Stopped herself before she sounded desperate or worse. "But you don't, so there's no point going down that path of self-destruction."

"I never meant to hurt you." He blinked, and Jacinta wondered if she saw a hint of wetness in his eyes. Hers were welling up and she fought for control.

"It'll be better this way. For both of us. I… I'll let you finish your dinner in peace."

Jacinta rose and went into kitchen. She dumped her food into the trash, put the plate in the dishwasher and went upstairs. Closing her bedroom door, she wiped away the tears and willed him to come after her.

But she knew he wouldn't, and that one last sliver of held-out hope began to sob when he didn't. She retrieved a suitcase and began putting things she'd need inside. The repetitive action of packing didn't ease the pain coursing through her, but being productive helped her feel that at least she was taking steps in the right direction. She'd meant what she said.

She wanted it all. And if Micah didn't love her and never would, then it was time to take charge and leave him behind.

After Jacinta retreated to her bedroom, Micah discovered he couldn't sleep. To fight his insomnia, he spent most of the night outside. He went for a long swim, doing lap after lap until his body ached. Afterward, he sat on an outdoor couch and listened to the lull of the pool's water feature. He drank two fingers of bourbon. Nothing helped him find peace. When he'd woken up in the morning after what seemed like two hours of sleep, he'd discovered Jacinta had left. He'd showered and met his siblings for a breakfast meeting.

He felt like crap and he looked it, too. A fact Vivienne

remarked on immediately. "What happened to you? You look like something the cat dragged in."

Micah exhaled a big breath. Might as well get the earth-shattering announcement over with. They'd find out soon enough. "Jacinta's moving out this weekend. She's calling it quits. I'm not sure if we'll stay married the full year or not. She's leaving that up to me."

Vivienne's accurate blame came swiftly. "What did you do?"

"I…" How did one admit to his siblings that he'd told Jacinta he didn't love her and never would? That he'd said he'd closed his heart?

Vivienne gave Micah a disappointed shake of her head. "You are such an idiot. Man, I'd love to knock some sense into your thick skull. You have the perfect woman as your wife and she loves you for you, and you're driving her away because of your own foolishness and stupidity."

"Yeah, that about sums it up." He chewed on his lips, alternating between dragging his teeth over his top lip and then the bottom. The motion made him think of Jacinta, who had a similar quirk, and then his mind remembered the time he'd painted her lips with chocolate, leading to their first lovemaking. Anguish pierced his soul. "She said I'm broken, and she's right."

Vivienne smacked her palms on the conference table so hard the pens in the center bounced. "Oh my God. Enough. You got cheated on and lied to about a baby that never existed. You were treated like crap by a former flame. Yeah, it broke your pride and your heart. But guess what? It's time to get over it. Yeah, that's harsh, but you're letting one moment in your life ruin the best thing that's ever happened to you. Stop giving your ex power. Take it back."

Vivienne drew a quick breath and plunged ahead. "Stop

being so afraid. You know, when I was younger, I always looked up to you. I found you so brave. Remember the rattlesnake? Remember how you killed it and saved me from being bitten? I worshipped you as any little sister might. And yeah, you scared off some of my boyfriends, but you were right about them." She pinned him with the glare she'd long perfected, the one that could make the toughest ranch hands quake in their boots. "Where's that guy? Where's the one who takes charge? Who makes lesser men tremble? Who held the thief at gunpoint? Whoever he was, he wouldn't let a little thing like maybe getting his feelings hurt stand in his way. Find him fast. Because this you sucks."

Micah glanced at Drake.

"What she said," his brother said, both palms held out in a "I'm not getting into this" gesture. Then he dropped his arms and shrugged. "But on second thought, yeah, not only is our sister right, but the truth is that you love Jacinta, so maybe it's time to stop being so stubborn and admit that."

"I don't." But the words didn't roll off his tongue. They'd first gotten caught in the back of his throat, as if he didn't really mean them.

"So you'd be okay with me asking her out?" Drake asked. "Because I think she's hot and I could use—"

Micah's response came out harsh and fierce, as if he were a bear growling. "Not if you want to live."

His brother leaned back in the chair and crossed his arms, his expression smug. "Then admit you love her. Because you sure sound like someone who can't stand the idea of her being with anyone else."

The thought of Jacinta marrying anyone else filled Micah with dread. Rage even. He wanted to be the one she woke up next to. He wanted to hold her in his arms until they were both old and gray, surrounded by their children and grandchildren.

He hated the fact she was moving out. Last night her words had cut him to the quick. She'd even given him a pass, saying she'd been the one who'd fallen in love when she knew he couldn't return the feelings.

But that fact was that he could. He'd simply been denying his feelings because he hadn't wanted to give Jacinta the power to hurt him. And in turn, he'd instead hurt her deeply. He'd asked her to compromise her integrity. And she'd found it and stood firm on her decision. He admired gumption. Hated the idea she was leaving. Was a fool if he let her go.

"Fine. I love her." The words burst forth with raw power and, as they did, Micah realized how true they were. He loved Jacinta and everything about her, from her smile, to her laugh, to her drive and ambition, to her kind and generous and loving heart. And she loved *him*. She was a gift, and he'd tossed it aside without hesitation because he'd been too afraid to let her in. He needed to be brave, to risk it all and put his heart on the line. "I love her."

"Thank goodness you admit it." Drake sighed. "Now, for your sake and all of ours, fix it. Because you've been a real pain in the ass this last week."

"She wouldn't believe me," Micah said. His pride and idiocy had probably cost him the best thing that had ever happened to him. "I screwed up. I hurt her. That's unforgivable."

"Then you'll need to show her that you love her and prove it to her. Show her you're sorry and how wrong you were," Vivienne urged. "Grovel. Come up with the grand gesture. Be a romantic. But whatever you do, don't let her get away. She loves you."

And he loved her. Micah's brain became a kaleidoscope of colors as idea after idea bombarded him. He rose to his feet. "If you'll excuse me, I think I need to leave this meeting. I've got important things to do…"

Drake grinned. "I'll text your assistant and tell them to cancel your appointments for the day."

"Thanks." Micah strode out of the meeting and drove to his house. He loved Jacinta. He wanted her forever, until the world ceased. He didn't want her to leave, to move her stuff out. He wanted her to stay and build a life with him. She was his heart. His soul. His other half. He could see the future clearly, as if the dark rain clouds of his past had parted to reveal the clear blue sky of the future. That was if he could convince her to give him a second chance.

To do that, he had to prove he loved her. Mere words wouldn't do. He was a man of action, and he had one shot to get this right. Luckily he knew exactly where to start.

Jacinta hadn't seen Micah at the office all day. After the previous night, she'd wanted to check on him and make sure he was okay. Even if she was leaving, she still cared for him and she had dropped quite the bombshell. But when she'd looked for him, his assistant had told her Micah had cancelled his entire day and wasn't coming in. Her replacement had no idea where her husband was. Jacinta had sent Micah a text message, but he hadn't responded and he had his read receipts turned off. When she'd texted her friends and asked what they thought about Micah's disappearance, she'd gotten back three separate shrugging emojis. Kim had even added, He's a big boy. He's fine.

But Jacinta still worried. She loved him, and those emotions didn't shut off simply because she was leaving behind their real-in-name-only marriage. Jacinta gritted her teeth and then unclenched her jaw. Kim was right. Jacinta had to do what was best for her. Even if what she was about to tell her abuela would hurt both of them. With this in mind, she drove the crossover to her grandmother's, arriving right on time. As she parked, she patted the wheel. She'd hate giving the car back but, like the money, she wouldn't keep the car either. As she stepped onto the porch, Abuela opened the door and the aroma of delicious food wafted to Jacinta's nose. She sniffed. "Are you making your famous chicken casserole?"

"I am."

Her grandmother rarely made the time-consuming dish, saving it for special events. "What's the occasion? You know, doesn't matter. Smells delicious and I could use a good home-cooked meal." Jacinta followed her grandmother into the kitchen.

Abuela cocked her head. "You look a little worse for the wear," she observed. "Bad day at work?"

"I didn't sleep much last night." Jacinta set her purse next to Abuela's.

Her grandmother sent her a knowing glance. "Your husband is keeping you busy, eh? He's a good one, that Micah. I didn't think so at first, but he's growing on me."

Micah was awesome. But he wasn't the problem or the reason she hadn't slept well. "Abuela, there's something you should know…"

Abuela waved a finger. "Don't tell me you two are having problems already. It's been what? A week? Don't you realize all marriages have issues? The key is to work at them, work *through* them. Is yours so broken you can't fix it?"

Without waiting for an answer, Abuela opened the oven and removed the baking dish. She set it on a cooling rack and steam wafted skyward. Then, placing the pot holders aside, she turned and studied Jacinta. "Then again, perhaps you and Micah did marry too fast. Did you make a mistake? Is he not good enough for you? Do you not love him?"

"My loving him isn't the problem." Micah had captured her whole heart, but their situation had broken it into pieces. "It's the fact that he doesn't love me."

"Ah." Abuela sighed. "Are you sure about that? That was a pretty expensive wedding you two threw. My dress came from the department store. But your dress…" Abuela shook her head before she said anything critical about the extravagance. "No man opens his pocketbook like that if he doesn't feel something."

"I wish that were true." Micah's attempt to please her was one reason the situation was so painful and why she was there. "He's rich. He can afford to throw money around."

"But is he the kind of man who *does* toss it about? Would he be the same person if he didn't have his billions?"

"I'd like to believe so." Micah was generous and kind and thoughtful. All reasons she loved him.

"Then there's part of your answer." Abuela turned off the oven. She reached for a tall glass and pressed it against the water dispenser on the refrigerator. Clear liquid streamed until she withdrew the glass. "Help me understand the rest. If he didn't love you, then why did he marry you?"

Jacinta's explanation wrenched out on a cry of despair. "Because you gave me an ultimatum. Because I wanted to run the business. Because I couldn't stand letting the company go to Sofia and her selling it. Micah was doing me a favor. Abuela, my marriage to Micah…it's real in name only. We got married so I could keep the chocolate business. I couldn't bear the idea of losing it, of letting you down. I know how much the company means to you, to our family."

Abuela set the glass aside and drew Jacinta into a tight

embrace. "You could never let me down. But the business, even though I love it, is not worth sacrificing your happiness. That's all I've ever wanted for you. I may have pushed you toward marriage, but it was because I wanted you to find the same love and partnership that I had with your abuelo. The kind of love that lasts a lifetime. The business was a way to keep his memory alive and share our love and passion with friends. I always hoped that, one day, you would find someone to share that with, too. It was my dream for your cousin. My dream for you. My greatest wish is that you'd be happy forever with a soulmate."

She stroked Jacinta's hair. "But I realize now that I can't force that kind of love. It has to come naturally, in its own time. And if Micah isn't the one, then I must trust that you'll find your true partner when the time is right. But you love him, don't you?"

"I do. But that doesn't matter. Please forgive me for the lie. I've brought the papers." Jacinta moved out of her embrace and withdrew them from her oversized purse. "Give the company to Sofia. I don't care. I'll make sure to take care of you. But I can't live a lie anymore."

Abuela made no move to reach for the documents. "You mean you can't live with a man who doesn't love you."

"We married under false pretenses. I can't keep lying to people, most of all you. And even Sofia. I should show her more grace, be kinder perhaps. Dan's always gone and leaving her alone."

"She does have a lot going on, her own problems to handle. I hope someday you get closer, because family is what matters," Abuela said.

"I'm learning that," Jacinta admitted quietly. Everyone had their own problems, and as Abuela said, family was what mattered. Jacinta had simply wished that family had included Micah. "I want to clear the air. No more living a lie. I can't be in a marriage that's not real."

Her grandmother planted a hip against the counter. "Those vows seemed pretty real to me. Even if neither of you said that you loved the other directly. I was listening. I know what I heard in the tones each of you used. Sometimes things are unsaid but still spoken clearly. Have you asked him how he feels?"

That was the heart of the matter, and Jacinta's nod came out on a sob. "He's told me his heart was closed. He'll never love me. I can't live a life without love. I was wrong to think so."

"Maybe his heart will open. Maybe he'll come to his senses. You gave him what? A year? And you're ready to quit?"

"It's torture to love him and not be loved in return. I deserve to have a soulmate. Isn't that what you wanted for me? I'd hoped it was him, but..." Jacinta wiped her eyes as anguish made the words break off. She waved the papers at her grandmother. "Take back your business. I didn't marry for the right reasons and so I don't deserve it. I'll start over. Find something else to do, somewhere else to work. It's a fruitless effort to love someone who doesn't love you. I want what you and Abuelo had. What my parents had. No business is worth living without love."

"I shouldn't have been so rash in forcing you to marry. All I wanted was for you to find love." Abuela set the empty glass in the sink.

"I thought I had. But I can't force him to fall in love me." Jacinta put the papers on the counter. "Here. Take them."

Abuela made no move to retrieve the documents. Instead, she folded her arms and waited. Jacinta's forehead creased and awareness prickled. She'd never told her grandmother that she was marrying for a year. Suspicion crept in.

"You're taking this far too calmly. It's like you already knew this was going to happen, what I was going to say. That I was marrying for the wrong reasons. That it was a business deal."

"I had my worries. But I could tell you were falling in love with him." Her grandmother tilted her head twice to the right, indicating the hallway. "And he already filled me in on the rest."

"What?" Jacinta turned toward the doorway.

"I told her the rest." Micah entered.

He appeared haggard, as if he'd had a rough day, week… year. Her heart pounded. She wanted to go to him and gather him into her arms, but she stayed rooted. "Are you okay? What are you doing here?"

Lines creased a forehead she'd smoothed many times. "I couldn't let you throw away your future, *our* future."

It was as if her heart sat on a scale, tilting between overflowing with love or breaking into more pieces as she tried to determine his reasons. Whatever they were, they were too late.

"I've already told her that we married for the business. That our union wasn't real." Saying the words hurt worse than seeing him and knowing he'd never love her.

"Yes. He told me the reasons for your marriage this morning," Abuela said. "That's why I didn't appear surprised. His confession came far earlier than yours."

"I don't understand." Jacinta glanced between Abuela and Micah. He had dark, upset circles beneath his eyes. "Why did you tell her?"

"Because she needed to hear the truth from me. That the marriage was my idea. That, deep down, I might not have understood my own motivations. That I'd realized I'd be the biggest fool if I let you go, especially since I realized an earth-shattering truth today."

"What truth?" The scale began to tip again as hope bubbled.

"The truth is that you matter to me more than anything else in the world. I've already told your grandmother how I feel about you. Now I'm telling you, and since I doubt you'll believe me, I'm going to spend the rest of my life proving how much I care about you. How much I love you."

Had she hear him correctly? "What exactly are you saying? You love me?" She turned to Abuela. "What is going on?"

Her grandmother placed a gentle hand on Jacinta's arm. "What's going on is that you're not moving back in here. You're going to listen to what he has to say and then we're all going to sit down and eat dinner. I'll let you two have some privacy." With that, Abuela walked out of the room.

Micah crossed the kitchen in two strides. He hovered close but didn't intrude into her personal space. "Can you forgive me? Can you please give me another chance to prove that I'm the man for you? That I'm your soulmate? I love you, Jacinta. I know words are meaningless after how I've hurt you, but I'm going to show you that I mean them every day from now until forever if that's what it takes for you to believe me. You've wormed your way through the wall I'd built around my heart, and that's scary. It gives you the power to hurt me."

"I wouldn't." Her heart filled with love. "Never intentionally."

His tender gaze held hers. "I know. But irrational fear made me do something dumb, which was to tell the woman that I love that I didn't. The moment I realized that you were leaving was the most painful thing I'd ever experienced. I asked myself, if my heart was so closed, like I believed, why did I hurt so much? And, as cheesy as it sounds, it was like the blinders came off. I was in pain because I loved you. I hurt because you are my sun, my light, my life. You gave me a sonnet at the wedding. I'll give you the words of my childhood. I love you to the moon and back and then to beyond infinity."

Tears began streaming down Jacinta's face as she realized he meant every word, even if he had them a bit jumbled. "You're serious."

He risked reaching for her hands and took them in his. "As a heartbeat." He placed her palm against his chest so she could feel the thump-thump that beat for her. "I love you. Please come home so I can show you how much."

Jacinta's answer was to launch herself into his arms. She captured his lips with a kiss that promised everything. Dreams did come true, for his love was the fulfillment of every hope she'd ever had for the future. "I love you," she said, her hands planted on his chest.

"And I love you. Always and forever."

They were still kissing when Abuela returned to the kitchen. She reached into a drawer and removed some aluminum foil. "I see you worked things out."

Micah held Jacinta in his arms, her back pressed against his front as they smiled at her grandmother. "We did." Jacinta beamed. "Good thing I never took off my rings." A matching band had joined the beloved engagement ring.

Abuela nodded. "Remember this lesson. Your marriage may have temporary trials and bumps in the road, but your love will always prevail if you tackle things together. You are stronger when you work as one unit, and no one can miss the way you feel about each other. You are soulmates."

Using the end of the aluminum foil box, she nudged the papers back across the counter. "You have my business with my blessing, *mi querida*. I can't wait to hear about what you do with it. Although, I'm suspecting that you'd like to wait and tell me about it tomorrow as you have other more important places to be."

"Yeah, if you don't mind," Micah said, his arms wrapped around Jacinta's waist so that they clasped and rested on her stomach. "Can we take a rain check on dinner?"

"Take it with you." Abuela covered the casserole dish and placed it into a carrier. "I have a feeling you'll need substance. Now, kiss me goodbye and get out of here. Shoo. I believe you promised me grandchildren."

Micah and Jacinta ate the delicious casserole much later, straight from the pan, after a long bout of sealing their love in the most intimate way possible.

Jacinta forked a bite into his mouth and he returned the favor.

"Thank you for loving me," Micah said.

"Thank you for making an honest woman out of me," Jacinta returned softly. "I love you."

"You were always honest. I was the one lying to myself about how much I love you." He sipped some water. "I never believed I'd be able to say those words to anyone and now they are slipping off my tongue with ease. You've changed me for the better."

"You weren't too bad before. Just somewhat misguided." She waved her empty fork.

His smile was so full of love it made her heart overflow with joy. "Well, I'm on the right path now. I can't believe how lucky I am."

"You are a Fortune," she teased.

"As are you, Mrs. Fortune." He dropped a kiss on her nose. "The love of my life. My wife. I like the sound of that. *My wife*. My love."

"Should we tell your family that everything's okay?" He'd told her earlier about the meeting with his siblings.

Micah plucked the fork from her fingers and set the casserole pan aside. He drew her into his arms. "We can tell them tomorrow. When they don't hear from us, they're smart enough to figure it out, especially as they knew I was going to go find you. Right now, I have other things on my mind, like proving to you exactly how much I love you. I'm planning on showing you how our love is going to last forever."

Since she loved him to the heavens and beyond, and would until the end of their days, Jacinta showed him right back.

* * * * *

Don't miss the next installment of the new continuity
The Fortunes of Texas:
Secrets of Fortune's Gold Ranch

To Catch a Fortune
by Rochelle Alers

On sale June 2025, wherever Harlequin
books and ebooks are sold.

And catch up with the previous titles in
The Fortunes of Texas:
Secrets of Fortune's Gold Ranch

Faking It with a Fortune
by USA TODAY *bestselling author Michelle Major*

A Fortune's Redemption
by USA TODAY *bestselling author Stella Bagwell*

A Fortune with Benefits
by Jennifer Wilck

Available now!